ALWAYS THE MATCHMAKER

Never the Bride
Book 8

Emily E K Murdoch

ARE YOU SIGNED UP FOR DRAGONBLADE'S BLOG?

You'll get the latest news and information on exclusive giveaways, exclusive excerpts, coming releases, sales, free books, cover reveals and more.

Check out our complete list of authors, too!

No spam, no junk. That's a promise!

Sign Up Here

www.dragonbladepublishing.com

Dearest Reader;

Thank you for your support of a small press. At Dragonblade Publishing, we strive to bring you the highest quality Historical Romance from the some of the best authors in the business. Without your support, there is no 'us', so we sincerely hope you adore these stories and find some new favorite authors along the way.

Happy Reading!

CEO, Dragonblade Publishing

Additional Dragonblade books by Author Emily E K Murdoch

CHAPTER ONE

S HE PROMISED NOT to cry. It was foolish. Miss Theodosia Ashbrooke attended so many weddings every year that attempting not to cry went against her sensibilities.

Especially when it was one of *her* weddings.

"Charles and Priscilla have consented together in holy wedlock, and have witnessed the same before God and this company," the vicar said, smiling benevolently, "and thereto have given and pledged their troth, and have declared the same by giving and receiving of a ring, and by joining of hands, I pronounce that they be man and wife, together."

The happy couple beamed as Theodosia held a lace handkerchief to hide the tears threatening to pour at any moment.

How could she help it? Another wedding, another success, and all thanks to her careful and delicate matchmaking skills. The bride may never know the full extent of her interference this time, not being officially a client, but still...

Theodosia smiled as the newlyweds took their seats in the pew before her, ready to listen to the marital sermon. Charles had no idea what was good for him, the fool—despite being the Duke of Orrinshire. He would never have realized his affections for Miss Seton if it not for her delicate maneuvering.

Sometimes Miss Ashbrooke's matchmaking service was so good, one did not even need to be paying her to gain a happily ever after.

1

"Dearly beloved, marriage is a holy thing," the vicar said in a slow, smiling voice. "And yet it reminds us, of course, of the harmony intended between God and His Church. When we read…"

Theodosia sighed and immediately stopped listening. She was hardly a heathen, but after fourteen weddings this year, she had heard almost every variation of the wedding sermon and was probably qualified enough to give one of her own.

She glanced around the church. Packed to the rafters, as one would expect for a lady so well respected as Miss Seton and a gentleman so well known as Charles Audley, the Duke of Orrinshire, there were some new faces to Theodosia.

All the better. Many of the ladies were quite pretty and of eligible age. Theodosia's fingers itched to retrieve her notebook from her reticule immediately but would wait until the wedding reception. She would have plenty of time there to examine ladies for their suitability—not that her requirements were that high, at present. If she were to find Lord Rust's nephew a bride, she would need to find at least three more.

Inspiration struck, and Theodosia leaned forward to tap the bride gently on the shoulder. At first, Priscilla did not move. After several more delicate taps on her shoulder, still nothing.

"Miss Seton!" whispered Theodosia, ensuring her voice did not carry above the tones of the reverend. "Miss Seton!"

The bride turned her head just enough to catch the matchmaker's gaze. "You of all people, Miss Ashbrooke, should know better than to address me with my maiden name!"

The whisper carried, but Theodosia was bold enough to ignore the looks it attracted. One had to be far craftier when a matchmaker.

"Tosh, you are a maiden still," she whispered, noting with interest the scarlet blush that seared the bride's cheeks. "Now, tell me. Do you know of any eligible young ladies you can introduce me to?"

It had not occurred to Theodosia that her request was anything but a polite inquiry, and the vicar glared and raised his voice as he continued.

"And so that means, of course…"

The bride was giggling, but this did not deter her, naturally. A matchmaker could not simply halt her pursuit of other people's happiness after a little laughter.

Lowering her voice to avoid the ire of the vicar, Theodosia whispered, "I have far too many gentlemen on my books, and although with a few good matches the balance could be utterly changed, I—"

"Miss Ashbrooke," murmured the groom without looking away from the vicar, "if you are not quiet, I will have you removed."

Theodosia's mouth fell open. And after all she had done for him, extricated him from one foolish engagement and helped him to secure a second, a much happier one—to be so treated!

Well, that was gratitude for you. Theodosia frowned and leaned back in her seat. That was a lesson learned at any rate. If the rich and titled wished to gain her services, she would require them to pay like any other client.

And there was still the reception. The Dowager Duchess of Orrinshire had simply invited anyone who was anyone, Theodosia had heard—and she always heard the gossip about weddings. It was her trademark.

After all, why would one engage a matchmaker for one's son or daughter if the matchmaker was not entirely up to date with the latest engagements and fashionable styles?

The reception it was, then. She would speak to the guests there— delicately, of course. Anyone who decided to contract Miss Theodosia Ashbrooke to find them a partner for life could not only be guaranteed that happy ending but, naturally, discretion.

The joyous couple and their entourage swept down the aisle, and Theodosia joined the back of the crowd as they exited the church and stepped into the sunshine. Smiles were on every face.

Weddings. They brought out the best in people, every time. How many familial disagreements had been ended at a wedding— sometimes thanks to the bride and groom themselves? How many warring friends were brought together in bridal parties? How many new friends made in the pews of a wedding?

Theodosia grinned. She could imagine nothing better than her life, living from invitation to invitation, with the warm knowledge that most of them were due to her ingenuity and introductions.

Her heart faltered only slightly as she watched Charles sweep his bride in his arms and kiss her most devotedly.

Nothing better, save that.

But a matchmaker did not receive proposals. She orchestrated them.

It was but a short walk to Orrinspire Park, and the wedding reception was in full flow by the time Theodosia reached it.

"And I was astonished to hear that Miss Frances Lloyd does not mind the marriage at all!" someone was saying in an astonished voice. "Really! She was engaged to the Duke in the first place, as you know, but now…"

The voice died away as Theodosia continued to walk through the large hallway, all white stone and marble, but other voices rose in their turn.

"—arranged marriages are very old hat," said a gentleman wisely to his companions. "I believe we are seeing the end of them. Why, only last week…"

"Yes, that's what I said, an arranged marriage!" A young lady blushed at Theodosia's gaze and continued in a low voice, "I mean, I thought those had died out with our grandparents!"

Theodosia smiled. Arranged marriages may have had their heyday; that was true. Just look at the way Charles Audley had rebelled against his mother's insistence that Theodosia find him a bride.

But *matched* marriages? Betrothals in which both the husband and wife are looking for the same things, are compatible in every important way, and most critically, have a devastating attraction for one another?

Her smile rose. Matched marriages would surely never be unwelcome. She excelled at creating them, for a start, and she had more godchildren from her happiest matches than she knew what to do with at Christmastide.

"Miss Ashbrooke!"

Theodosia turned to see Mr. and Mrs. Needham, smiling arm in arm. It was always wonderful to see happy clients.

"Miss Ashbrooke, how are you?" Mr. Needham said, reaching out to shake her hand.

She allowed the indecorum. The Needhams were one of her greatest triumphs. "Very well, I thank you. And Mrs. Needham, you are well?"

"Absolutely blooming," she said with a dimpled smile. "You know, Miss Ashbrooke, we welcomed our third child into the family a few months ago."

"Third?" Theodosia could not help but look a little surprised. It had only been five years—no, less than five years—since the Needhams had wed. Three children in five years was impressive.

"Oh yes, and I don't think they could have been born into a happier family," said Mr. Needham, looking fondly at his wife. "I can never thank you enough, Miss Ashbrooke, for helping us find each other. You have done more for my joy than I can express."

Theodosia beamed. "It is nothing, I assure you. I am delighted to see your continued happiness, and it gives me much in return."

The Needhams bowed, still arm in arm, and walked away to greet another couple.

It was bittersweet, seeing such marital felicity. That was the problem being the matchmaker. Happy endings were not in short supply, but she did not receive one of her own. She was the one standing alone at a wedding reception with no one else to talk or dance with.

She walked gracefully, her skirts sweeping along the hardwood floors, into the room set up for dancers. Chairs had been placed around the room, and six or eight couples swirled around, laughter growing as the steps became more complicated.

Theodosia took a seat and watched the world go by. Footmen appeared at regular intervals to offer her biscuits, which she accepted eagerly, and glasses of wine, which she politely declined.

It would never do to lose her head when, later on in the evening's celebrations, she would circulate and find the lonely, isolated, and most importantly, the *single* young ladies who would happily accept a place on the books of society's greatest matchmaker.

It was almost time, Theodosia knew, to be considered a spinster. In a way, it would be a relief. Then no one would smile pityingly during her client appointments or ask carefully whether she had ever considered marriage for herself.

The world was always watching, and society never held back when it came to a single lady.

The thought passed through her mind as her gaze fell upon an elderly woman seated on the other side of the dancers. Theodosia sat for almost twenty minutes, and still, the lady stared but made no move to approach her.

She knew the signs, usually an older woman, often a widow as it was, in this case, judging by her deep purple gown. There was an interest in her, yes, but not enough bravery to approach her in public.

No, it was always her responsibility to make the first connection, and Theodosia sighed as she rose and straightened her gown. Business never waited, and she had long ago become accustomed to the strange ways that mothers went about finding spouses for their children.

Stepping around the dancing couples delicately, Theodosia had almost reached the other side of the room when she was distracted by a most miserable young lady.

"Miss—Miss Lymington, is it not?"

The lady looked up from her seat and quickly dashed away tears. "Yes?"

Theodosia smiled and pulled her handkerchief from her reticule. "Keep it."

Miss Lymington stared, reaching out for the handkerchief and using it to mop her eyes. "You are most kind, Miss…?"

"Ashbrooke," Theodosia said gently. "And I think you and I should have a conversation after this wedding. Here, my card. Tell your mother I would be happy to make an appointment to see you both."

She did not wait to answer any questions from the weeping Miss Lymington. She did not need to. Her card would invoke enough curiosity, and if she were not mistaken, she had just added an eligible young lady to her roster. More than eligible, pretty, and with a large dowry, if the *ton's* gossip was correct.

When she finally arrived at the side of the older woman who had been watching her so closely, Theodosia curtseyed.

"May I join you, my lady?"

The woman nodded without saying a word. Theodosia sat beside her, arranging her skirts to ensure her feet were covered, and waited.

She had never been hunting, but she had read about it and believed the general instincts were similar to her own business.

One waited.

It was a good five minutes before the woman eventually said, "I have a challenge for you."

Theodosia smiled, not taking her eyes from the dancers and the crowd of people starting to congregate in the doorway. "I have met many challenges in my time, none which have beaten me."

"You are proud," said the woman.

She considered this. "No," she said, after careful thought. "No, I just know my skills, and I know my worth. Few ladies do, but I have too much success to ignore it entirely."

The woman raised an eyebrow but still did not look around.

Theodosia smiled. *There was always one that needed further proof.* "I am the one who matched this wedding—one of fifteen this year. I know what I can do. I do it every day."

Only then did the woman smile. "You should have been a countess or a duchess."

The words stung, and Theodosia almost gasped aloud. *Could she— no, she could not possibly know.* It was a coincidence. They did happen.

Struggling to maintain her composure, she said, "Well, I am not. How can I help you, madam? Seeking a match?"

It was a little reckless, speaking so boldly, but Theodosia could not help it. There had to be a spark of rebelliousness in a matchmaker. How else did one connect those who would never have considered themselves suitable?

"'Tis not for myself!" the woman snorted. "My son. He is a true challenge."

Curiosity overwhelmed Theodosia's determination to be aloof, and for the first time in the conversation, she examined her companion more closely. Her impeccable memory threw up a name.

"I do apologize for not recognizing you immediately," she said with a smile, "Dowager Countess of Lenskeyn."

The dowager inclined her head but still did not grace Theodosia with the courtesy of looking at her.

She stared at the older woman, intrigue flowing through her mind. No one had seen the Earl of Lenskeyn for years—five years, maybe? Seven? He was not a recluse, not in the traditional sense, but he seemed to avoid polite society as though it was a curse on his name.

She could not recall the last time he was in town. The Continent, they said. That's where he was. But he seemed to have few friends to miss him and precious little family to petition for his presence. *Was there not a tragedy in the family just a week ago?*

Time to get to business. "I have a small fee," she said delicately. "A small token of appreciation, my clients consider it, just a—"

"I will pay double," interrupted the dowager countess.

Theodosia's eyebrows raised. Very few clients ever quibbled over her fee; that would be bad manners, and the last thing one wanted to do in the process of securing a matchmaker was to come across as miserly.

At the same time, few people looked forward to paying it. With about twenty matches made every year, Theodosia had to charge sufficiently high fees to live on.

The Lenskeyn family was wealthy, certainly. *But why double? Why was his mother so desperate to marry him off?*

As though able to read her mind, the dowager said quietly, "I need heirs, Miss Ashbrooke. My son grows old, and I grow older, and yet there are no heirs to the earldom."

Theodosia nodded. It was not a new story.

"I inherited the earldom through my father for my son," the elderly woman continued. "The line of the Lenskeyns runs through my veins, and I will not allow the family name to disappear. There may have been…children, you understand. My husband was not an honorable man. But not heirs. For a legitimate heir, my son needs a wife. Find him one."

Theodosia swallowed. This was all most irregular. She had usually met the son in question, or the daughter, depending on who was paying the fee and could estimate the level of difficulty that finding a partner for them would be.

Everyone had faults. She had seen too much of the world to think otherwise. But in the case of the Earl of Lenskeyn, she had no idea what faults she would be forced to look past or…well, improve upon.

Handsome or ill-featured? Charming or despicable?

It was impossible to tell. There was not even enough gossip about the earl to draw upon.

"My son. He is a true challenge."

Theodosia smiled. She could not turn down a challenge. She never had.

Nevertheless, it was against her better judgment that she said, "You know, my lady, I cannot make promises. Not every client of mine finds their true match immediately, and your son is...?"

"Near forty," said his mother with a sniff. "And double your fee may not be enough."

What was this man like? "You know exactly what to say to interest me, don't you?"

Finally, the Dowager Countess of Lenskeyn turned to look at her. Her face was wrinkled, and her eyes a soft blue with the same sharpness they had undoubtedly possessed fifty years ago.

It was an appraising look, and her words were direct when she spoke. "Miss Ashbrooke, it is clear to me you are plain but clever. You are precisely what my son needs. Coaching to become a better man. A matchmaker to find him a wife."

It was impossible not to feel offended at the woman's words, but Theodosia was not proud enough to argue. She had a little beauty, but it had already started to fade. She had no title, no wealth to recommend her, besides the small amount she had squirreled away for her pension.

"And that is what makes me an excellent matchmaker," she said. "You cannot have a pretty one."

The dowager graced her with another smile. "I knew we would understand each other, Miss Ashbrooke. So, will you accept my son as a client? A project?"

Theodosia hesitated. It went against her better judgment, accepting a client without even meeting him. The little his mother had said about him hardly recommended him to a matchmaker, and the doubled fee suggested his parent considered him twice as difficult to match.

She nodded. "I will."

The dowager nodded as she rose to her feet. "Good luck. You will need it."

CHAPTER TWO

ALBEMARLE HOWARD, EARL of Lenskeyn, sighed heavily as he looked around the stuffy, over-adorned rooms his mother had secured for the Season in Bath. Gold trimmings around the paintings, red velvet curtains with beads along the bottom, a carpet so deep his boots were rapidly disappearing...if he cut his mother in half, he would find *ostentatious* carved through her.

He would not have minded so much if the indulgence had been in the latest style. Grecian columns were very popular at the moment, and Albemarle had spent enough time in Greece to appreciate the architectural styling.

But as his gaze swept across the room, he saw none of the fashionable choices he had hoped for. No, it was all 1790s glamour, the style his mother had adored when he had been a child.

It felt like a lifetime ago. *It was a lifetime ago.*

Now his next birthday would be his fortieth, and he was beginning to feel...not old, exactly. Not even matured.

Left behind.

His back hurt if he slept on his stomach now, and he had more silver hairs than he would care to examine.

"I do not know why she wanted to meet me here," he said. "Or at all, for that matter."

His mother was not in the room to explain her strange plans. She had not yet appeared, and so instead, he spoke to the footman in their damned livery, all blue and yellow. *Like a canary.*

The man looked straight ahead without saying a word. *Utter passivity, just like the ruling classes,* Albemarle thought dully. It would not be long before he was back on the Continent, away from all this drudgery.

When had England become so…boring?

After another five minutes of waiting, the earl put his plate of cake down and started pacing about the room. Like a caged lion captured from the plains after years of ruling as king, he was stuck here.

He reached the window and watched the world go by. He was a dutiful son, in the main. At least, he considered himself a dutiful son. His mother said, "Do not get into mischief in London," so he went to the Continent for a decade. His mother said, "I need you back in the country," and he spent a year in Ireland with Patrick O'Leary. Good man. Viscount Donal was different, though. *Married.*

But today was perhaps her most specific demand. Meet her here, in her rooms, at eleven o'clock the next morning.

And here he was. It was impossible to refuse, and not just because the demand was written in her own hand. It was a strange summons, even for her. He had arrived with five minutes to spare, but now the clocks were chiming half past the hour, and he was getting impatient.

A gaggle of schoolboys swept along the street, hurried along by a schoolmistress who looked quite domineering, even from two floors up. A pair of gentlemen walked by, debating something hotly. *Politics, probably.*

And there was a lady. She stood on the other side of the street, a pocket watch in her hands. *Probably waiting for a friend to visit the shops on Milsom Street,* Albemarle thought.

Even she had something better to do than wait around here for his mother.

Despite himself, he smiled as he started pacing again. His mother always ensured she was late, even for her son. She always did whatever she wanted. Her superiority complex dwarfed the Regent himself.

"You are very quiet." The words were snapped out by the only person in the world who could order him about in the sure knowledge he would acquiesce.

"Yes, I am, Mother," Albemarle said quickly, falling back in the ridiculous armchair with more stuffing than a turkey.

The dowager countess swept around the room and stood, meaningfully, beside his armchair.

Albemarle sighed, rose, and kissed his mother on the cheek.

"I should think so," she said haughtily, but her lips curled up at the corners. "Now sit down, Albie, that's a good boy."

The good boy of almost forty years sat, lounging back as he beheld his mother. She had not seemed to age a day since he had last saw her—*what, a year ago?*

Whatever reason she had for summoning him, it was probably just one of those visits she demanded periodically because she missed him, a sentiment which always confused him.

He had invited her to Greece, not once but several times. She had refused to make the visit. They had met once, by appointment, in Paris. *A compromise*, he had said. *A damned cheek*, she had said.

"You look terrible," she said as she took her seat.

Albemarle smiled. "You always say that, and I never do."

Every so often, this happened. She would get worried about the family and demand to see her sons. If he were nearby—or on the same island, which essentially was the same thing—he would come, sit with her, and then be back on his way.

Elmore's death had hit her hard. The funeral had only been…what, a week ago? It felt like an age. No mother should bury her son.

Unaccustomed to seeing his mother twice in the same calendar year, let alone the same month, Albemarle shifted in his seat. He had nothing against her, obviously. *Damn fine woman.* But she was hardly the best companion.

"Hmm," his mother said, pouring a cup of tea and handing it to him without asking whether he wanted one. A plate of biscuits was between them. She did not offer them to him. "And how have you been, Albemarle? You may go."

This last sentence had been thrown at the footman who bowed, relieved to be given permission to escape.

As the door shut, the dowager countess snapped, "You have not told me how you are."

"I was waiting for the hired help to depart. I don't know where you find them, Mother," he said, drinking the lukewarm tea. "And I have been fine, thank you."

After pouring a cup of tea for herself, she looked at him critically. "And there isn't anything else?"

He sighed. It always went in this pattern—he was not even sure anymore why he bothered turning up. He knew the script and could probably fill in half her words to boot.

"What do you want to hear about, Mother? My gambling debts? The man I almost fought in a duel last week for his cheek? The woman I—"

"That is quite enough of that," his mother interrupted wearily. "You know I have no wish to hear about anything like that. Really, you are a most disagreeable child."

He grinned. "Apple doesn't fall far from the tree, Mother."

It was impossible to keep a mischievous tone from his voice. They shared the same opinion of his father, and it had been a relief to many, not just the family, that the man had died twenty years ago.

He reached for a biscuit and almost gagged. It was very dry. Taking a huge gulp of tea to force it down, he tried not to cough.

"I attended the wedding of Charles, Duke of Orrinshire, a few days ago."

Albemarle rolled his eyes. He did not need his mother to continue—now he knew precisely why he had been summoned, but no amount of complaining would do any good.

He was not going to roll over like a damned dog and simply accept a bride because his mother wanted him to have one.

"Oh, yes?" he replied as casually as he could. No point attempting to head her off the topic. Better to let her get it out of her system, and then they could return to conversation like rational beings.

"Yes," said his mother, her voice iron. "The bride was a Miss Priscilla Seton. Nice girl, I think. Good family."

He smiled. "I am very pleased for Orrinshire, then. You know, I heard of a scandal recently that I think you will like. 'Tis between Marnmouth, the Earl, you know, and—"

"I do not want to hear the gossip of others," she said, slamming her teacup onto its saucer. Tea seeped over the rim. "I want to create some gossip for ourselves—meaningful gossip. Albemarle Howard, you are the fourteenth Earl of Lenskeyn. You are almost forty! It is time you were married."

Albemarle's heart sank. Just another advancement in the campaign to force a bride upon him.

She wanted to marry him off, like some sort of...of woman!

"I thank you for your concern, Mother, but I have plenty of time," he began easily.

Her glare deepened. "You are almost forty, you foolish man. Do you really think you have that much time?"

It was at that moment his damned back gave a twinge. He had never given his age much thought. What was forty? Now he was starting to feel it. When a cold wind blew through Ireland, his bones knew a storm was coming.

"I do not feel old," he said defensively, a complete lie in the moment.

His mother snorted. "When I was your age, I had two sons and four daughters. What do you have?"

Albemarle smiled. "Debts, a mysterious reputation, and no ties to anyone, save yourself, Mother."

It was possible the look she gave him—a mixture of disapproval, disappointment, and disbelief—hid a smile.

"I should have known you would not take this seriously," she sighed. "You will have to eventually."

"I honestly do not see why."

She was not a woman easily beaten, but her voice cracked as she said, "Because my husband—your foolish father!—changed the entail, that's why."

The words rang out in the drawing room, and for the first time in the conversation, Albemarle leaned forward with interest.

"Ah, the old Lenskeyn entail," he grinned. "I think it was a rather good idea. No reason why, just because you did not have any brothers, that the line should go extinct. You carried the title through your bloodline and into me, your son."

His mother looked quite distressed now. "Yes, but that was the old entail."

"The old entail?" He had never heard of a change. "Why was I not told about this before?"

She glared. "When you live on this island for more than two minutes, *then* you can dictate what you should or shouldn't be told!"

The barb barely stung. Albemarle had no love for England—no hatred for it, either. It was just...*boring*. He wanted to see the world. Now he was back, and the entire way his title would descend had been altered?

"You are my only male heir, and you have no children. Your father..." His mother's voice trailed away for a moment as she collected herself.

Albemarle's features hardened. Neither of them had kind words to say about his father, and they had mutually agreed, years ago, to speak of him as little as possible.

"He changed the entail," she managed. "One of your sisters can no longer inherit the title for their sons. It has to be one of *my* sons, and that means you. If your brother had lived..."

Once again, her voice trailed away, the anger gone. She gave a huge sigh and covered her face with her hands, sobbing loudly. The iron dowager had been reduced to tears.

It was this emotion, rather than the barely concealed fury, that finally broke through Albemarle's armor.

"Damn it all, Mother, don't cry," he said quietly, fishing out his handkerchief and handing it over.

It took a few minutes for the older woman to collect herself, breathing slowly for a minute, before she could continue in a firm voice.

"If Elmore had lived, it would have been different. He was married. Why, his widow may even now be with child!"

Albemarle nodded. *Unlikely, but possible.* "I admit, I find it hard to believe he died only two weeks ago."

"Well, there it is," his mother said, irritably. "If she is with child, if she has a son, that will be different. We will have a Howard of the next generation, but if it is a girl…We need to wait and see, but until then, we need you to marry. One heir is not sufficient. We need more."

Albemarle shifted uncomfortably. Elmore was besotted with his wife. Everyone knew that. After five years of marriage, of waiting, of prayers, no child had come. Elmore had died just weeks ago, and he had barely considered what that would mean for him.

Heirs. Damn and blast, but he, a father?

"We need heirs," his mother repeated.

"No, *you* need heirs," he snapped, unable to help himself.

Her eyes sparkled. "Yes, *I* need heirs. 'Tis my title I have carried for you. If I could have more sons, I would, but the baton has been passed to you now. It is time for you to act like your title, like the privilege your name has accorded you, and look for a bride."

She was staring with such desperation that Albemarle actually considered the possibility. A bride. A wife. *A mother to his children?*

It was a heady thought, and though it conjured up some rather fanciful ideas about pleasure on tap, surely no amount of bedding could make up for the fact he would be tied down. One woman. One home. A family.

It was not for him.

One look at his mother told him, saying that outright was hardly a wise idea. He would not lie to the poor woman, but neither must he tell the absolute truth.

Humoring his mother was not the same as lying. She did not need to know he had no intention of marrying anyone.

There was a way out of this, if only he could find it.

"'Tis not as easy as all that, Mother," he said, testing the waters. "There are not as many eligible young ladies around, and then there is all the trouble of courting, wooing, and then the proposal—it is a lot of work."

"If you are about to try to tell me that finding a bride is as difficult as carrying and birthing a child," his mother said severely, "I recommend you desist."

Albemarle swallowed. *Well, that was probably fair.*

"But you must admit, I could spend all that time on a lady just to find that she has no serious intentions," he said.

The damned title. *What did he care for a title?* It could go to a cousin for all he cared—there were plenty of Howard cousins in the most fashionable homes in the country.

"Mother, I understand your desire to know where the title will go next," he said instead, trying a different tack. "I think it is probably easier to find a Howard cousin, and—"

"Do not worry yourself," she interrupted imperiously. "I have taken care of everything."

Albemarle's heart sank. That was an ominous phrase, especially from his mother. It was only then that something which had been nagging at the back of his mind finally came to the fore.

She was still holding his handkerchief, but now he examined her face more closely, it was clear she had not shed a tear.

"What do you mean, taken care of it?" he said suspiciously. "No, I am serious. I heard all about Orrinshire's two engagements, the nonsense and trouble he managed to land himself in. No arranged marriage, do you hear me? I would have thought his experience would have frightened you off that trick."

The doorbell rang, clanging through the rooms his mother had rented.

"Who could that be?" Albemarle wondered aloud.

She shrugged. "Probably some tradesman unable to find the back door. I am serious, Albemarle. I have no wish to have to look for a Howard cousin who has never deserved the title."

There were footsteps in the hall as he tried to think of another way of distracting his mother from her plans.

"Albemarle, are you listening to me?"

He was not. "Of course, Mother."

She glared, quickly seeing the lie. "I want you to promise me that you are going to look for a bride."

He never made promises lightly. A promise was a promise, and if one had no intention of keeping it, one should not make it.

"I want you to promise me that you are going to look for a bride."

Albemarle smiled. He liked looking at women. *Looking* was not the problem, nor was touching. He did not want to put a ring on any woman, but looking? Looking was fine.

There was a promise he could make, in all honor.

"I promise," he said thoughtfully.

The broad smile on his mother's face should have told him immediately that somehow, he had still been cornered.

"Excellent," she said briskly as the door to the hallway opened behind him. "You are precisely on time."

CHAPTER THREE

T HE INSTANT THAT Theodosia stepped inside the opulent room, she noticed four things.

First, the Lenskeyns wealth was old money, far older than any other client she had ever dealt with. This was going to be an important client, and if she could do well here, then perhaps earls and dukes would become her regular customers, rather than highlights once or twice a year.

Second, the dowager countess looked far too pleased to see her. No one ever looked that pleased to see Miss Theodosia Ashbrooke, matchmaker, and there was a self-satisfied grin on the older woman's face that made Theodosia uncomfortable.

Thirdly, that there was a large plate of biscuits in the room—her favorites.

Fourth and lastly, it was evident the dowager had not informed her son she was going to be arriving. There was no mistaking that look of surprise on his face—a face that was, Theodosia examined it critically, one of the most devilishly handsome she had ever beheld.

"God alive," he breathed, rising to his feet. "How many other prospective brides are outside? Is there a queue?"

Theodosia opened her mouth for a forceful reply, but she hesitated. As the Earl of Lenskeyn had risen, she had been given a full view of him, and he was, though she would never admit it, heart-stopping.

Tall, far taller than her, with broad shoulders and a smirk that seemed a little too knowing. There was something brooding about his forehead, a frown of concern, and a rough beard covered his cheeks and chin.

He bowed curtly. "Well, Mother, I said I would look for a bride, true enough. I had not expected you to have a line of potential Countess of Lenskeyns waiting outside. How many are there?"

He laughed, a short, bark of a laugh that showed his displeasure and irritation far better than any words could.

The jolt within Theodosia calmed. "You are worth lining up for, then?"

She had dispensed with all pleasantries and politeness. This was clearly a man who did not value them—or worse, expected them in others but would never deign to deliver them himself.

A man, in short, in need of training.

Her tone had worked, too. The frown deepened, and his mouth fell open as behind him, his mother laughed.

"You foolish boy, sit down and mind your manners," she said to the imposing earl of almost forty. "Of course, I do not expect you to marry Miss Ashbrooke, the very idea. She is your matchmaker."

Theodosia had not been invited to sit down, but then, this was hardly a typical social visit, and so she once again took matters into her own hands. Stepping around the room and seating herself next to the astonished earl, she smiled.

"How do you do, my lord?"

She had kept her voice level despite the misgivings she was already starting to feel. She should have known not to accept a gentleman onto her books without meeting him first. This had never been done before, and this was the result.

The earl had thrown himself back onto the sofa, examining her with a critical eye. Theodosia did not blink. She was accustomed to it. It was part of her trade.

All the same, the words of the dowager countess rankled. Why should it be obvious she was not designed to be a potential bride for this rude and unfashionable man?

Unfashionable, yes, but not ill-looking. Now she was closer, she breathed in that subtle masculine scent, saw the strength in his arms as he put them behind his head, saw the suggestion of hair at his throat...

Theodosia swallowed. It was easy, in his presence, to lose her head. His mother had been right about one thing; he would certainly be a challenge.

Forcing herself to stop thinking like a woman, she began to examine him with a critical, professional eye. It was surprising, she had to admit, that the Earl of Lenskeyn had not yet managed to find a bride. He was handsome with that brooding countenance that Lord Byron had made so attractive.

He had a title, something that most ladies desired, and if his mother was anything to go by, he had money. *So what was the problem?*

"Are you quite finished, miss?" he snapped.

Theodosia smiled. *Ah yes, that was it. Everything else.* "No, not yet. Please remain still."

Reaching for her reticule, she pulled out the one essential part of her business that she simply could not do without, her notebook.

It had been with her since the beginning. In fact, she would soon have to look for a new one; there were only about twenty pages left in this one, and there were scraps of paper pushed in at seemingly random intervals.

Without it, she would be useless. It was her memory, her thoughts, her examinations, her plans.

Opening it to a new page and pulling a pencil from its folds, she starting making notes.

Earl of L. is finely featured + title + fortune + mature

He snorted. Theodosia looked up from her notebook coldly, glaring until he both put his arms down and looked a little abashed.

She waited until he looked suitably embarrassed, smiled at him, and then continued.

Mother keen, Earl

Theodosia looked up once more and saw a face full of boredom.

Mother keen, earl not. Aloof, disengaged. Will require training.

After underlining the last sentence, she placed the pencil on that page and closed the notebook, leaving it on her lap as she smiled at the pair of them.

"My name is Miss Theodosia Ashbrooke, and I have been making successful matches for society for the last eight years," she said calmly.

"And unsuccessful ones for how many years?" interrupted the earl with a sneer.

Theodosia hardly blinked. These were common concerns, albeit expressed far more rudely than she was accustomed to.

"Of the one hundred and sixty-four matches I have made, three have ended in divorce due to infidelity of the husband, one due to infidelity of the wife, and one due to a lack of heirs provided in the first three years," she said smoothly. "Hardly things I could predict while making their matches. That leaves one hundred and fifty-nine couples happily married."

"There you go, Albemarle," said the dowager smartly. "You are so useless as a prospective husband I have had to find a professional."

Theodosia forced herself not to laugh. "Now, my lady, many people request my services despite being excellent prospects because—"

"Because their mothers are desperate for grandchildren—or as they call them, heirs?" snapped the earl.

"I am the matchmaker, not you," said Theodosia serenely, forcing her pulse to calm. *She would not be provoked by this infuriating man.* "I will find a match that is pleasing, both for you and your mother."

His mother smiled. "That is very good of you, Miss—"

"I have no wish to please my mother." The earl's voice was petulant, even childish.

Theodosia sighed. *There would need to be a great deal of work on this one.*

"I can see that," his mother said tartly. "But you must marry, and whoever becomes your bride must fit the family. We cannot have you wed just anyone."

"Indeed, a common concern for the nobility of your rank," Theodosia said. *Perhaps a little flattery would get her further with this infernal man.* "I have often found—"

"Oh, stop it, we're impressed enough as it is," snapped the earl.

His glare was furious, and even Theodosia, inured as she had thought over a hundred gentlemen who she had helped, found herself a little ruffled. She had never met anyone quite so...well, *combative.* Even some of the majors she had aided had not been so irritable.

"References?" he barked.

Theodosia wordlessly pulled out the sheaf of references she kept at the front of the notebook, but instead of handing them to him, she smiled and passed them to his mother.

The dowager caught her eye, and there was a slight curve of her lip, just for a fraction. Then it was gone as she started to examine them.

The earl sniffed. "I've heard your name before, at any rate, Miss Ashbrooke, matchmaker. Yes, I have heard of you, miss, and it was not all good. You were involved in that Orrinshire scandal, weren't you?"

His voice had a teasing air, and it produced the effect he was doubtless seeking. Theodosia felt her cheeks flush.

Of course, he would have heard of that particular case.

Thankfully, her voice remained calm as she replied, "I am flattered, my lord, that you have recalled my name in relation to that *success.* Yes, I arranged the marriage of the Duke of Orrinshire to Miss Priscilla Seton, a woman of great wit and fortune. I still have Miss Frances Lloyd on the books, however, if you would like to meet her."

"This is not a cattle market!" he retorted, his dark eyes flashing.

"No," Theodosia replied, matching his fury, "I quite agree. We are organizing the next generation of the ruling class. I would say that needs to be done carefully and by a professional."

The earl stared, evidently at a loss to understand why she was so inconvenient as to disagree with everything. He turned to his mother, and Theodosia was relieved to see she was nodding approvingly.

"Miss Ashbrooke understands exactly what we are looking for," she said imperiously.

The earl snorted. "What *you* are looking for. I have no wish to be married, and I wish you would write that down in your damned notebook, Miss Ashbrooke."

Theodosia raised an eyebrow. "You do surprise me, my lord. Why, you are almost forty years of age, by my calculations."

She had known it was a low blow, but she was provoked. *Why was it that earls and dukes always thought they could speak to anyone exactly how they pleased? No thought for consequences, no thought for the feelings of others...*

It was time the Earl of Lenskeyn was shown what it was like to be spoken to in this way. She would match fire with fire.

"By God, *you think?*" He smiled, though there was no joy in his look. "And just how old are you, pray?"

"Albemarle Howard, you will not speak to a guest of mine in that way," began his mother, feathers ruffled.

Theodosia had not looked away. "Nine and twenty," she said calmly.

Now it was his turn to raise an eyebrow. "Then, should we not be more worried about *your* marriage prospects?"

Theodosia examined him closely. He was attempting to force a reaction, that much was clear. Reactionary. Rebellious for the sake of drama. *Interesting.*

Opening up her notebook and ignoring his outraged sounds of shock, she reviewed her notes so far.

Beginning a new line, she wrote:

Rude, bad-tempered, determined to get his way—interrupter. Rebellious for the sake of displeasing his mother.

Closing the notebook with a snap, she smiled and said, "That is very thoughtful of you, my lord, but your mother is not paying me to find a husband, but to find a bride for you. Now, any particular requests?"

He laughed at this, and his eyes seemed brighter, more focused. Theodosia became aware suddenly that they were seated on the same sofa when he leaned toward her.

"My God," he breathed. "Can you have one made to order?"

He really was most irritating.

"No," she sighed, maintaining her humor. "But knowing your preferences will permit me to present you with potential suits more aligned with your wishes."

She studied him, looking for any more positive features that she could use to find him a prospective bride.

He did not lack in positives. His clothes were modern, well kept. He was not portly nor thin. If his manners were anything to go by, he could be charming, and he was evidently relaxed in her company.

He caught her gaze, and a wicked grin crept across her face. He was arrogant, overly confident, and even a little brash.

Theodosia's smile became more natural. No wonder he had not yet wed, even at his age. *No woman could surely stand to be with him for more than five minutes.*

"My perfect woman," he mused. "Well, Miss Ashbrooke, let me see. Beautiful, rich, titled. Is that enough for you to be getting on with?"

Theodosia glanced at the dowager countess.

"God's teeth, you don't mean to tell me my mother gets a say?"

His mother expanded like a ruffled chicken. "Let me tell you, my boy—"

"Yes, she does," Theodosia interjected, attempting to soothe both mother and son. "Not just because my fee is coming from *her* purse, but because in my eyes, your mother is the head of your house."

The earl snorted. "A woman? Oh, no offense, Mother."

"A woman," repeated Theodosia.

"Now you see the challenge before you," said the dowager countess, still a little disgruntled. "What do you think?"

Theodosia did not answer immediately. He was certainly a challenge, more than she had ever faced before. She was not totally immune to his charms, and there was potential. But his manners got in the way of those good looks and the noble stock from which he came.

Standing up, she started to walk slowly around him. The earl, as she had suspected, did not watch her but sat in stony silence.

"Well, I can see the problem," said Theodosia briskly. "And I believe my first assessment from the moment of entering this room was correct. He will need training."

"Training?" he protested.

His mother was nodding. "I thought he would. All I have attempted through the years have come to naught, and even I have not been able to improve him past the age of two and twenty. That is why I came to you."

The earl looked outraged. "I do not need training!"

Theodosia stepped slowly around the back of the sofa, her critical eye roving over his form. "Posture, clarity of thought, temper—"

He whirled around and shouted, "I do not have a temper!"

Theodosia waited patiently to see whether he had anything else to say, and then said calmly, "Of course not."

Her response was enough to color his cheeks, and he turned back around to face his mother in silence.

"But if you do not mind me saying so, my lord," she offered as she returned to the front of the sofa, looking him straight in the eyes, "you are a rude, arrogant, and frankly a grating man with little to recommend you, save your wealth and title—I assume there is money?"

She had shot the last part at his mother, who nodded. Turning back to the earl, she saw his mouth had fallen open.

"Now, I am not a miracle worker, my lord, I am a matchmaker," said Theodosia with a smile. *She always liked this bit.* When she showed a man she was not just a skirt playing at weddings. She was a force to be reckoned with, and he would face a reckoning. "The best come to me, and that means I can find you the best."

"I do not need a damned matchmaker," he growled.

Theodosia allowed herself a short laugh. "You have not done well on your own so far."

"That is because I have no desire to marry!"

"That is not for you to decide," she shot back. Her heart was racing, and if she was honest with herself, she was enjoying this. "Your mother has decided, and that is what is going to happen."

The earl glared at his mother, who merely smiled.

Theodosia walked delicately past him and returned to her seat. "The challenge is not whether I can find you a bride, my lord. The question is whether you can keep her. And that is why training starts tomorrow."

His face was a picture of shock, his eyes wide and his mouth open.

"T-Tomorrow?" he spluttered.

"Oh, that is a shame," his mother said. "We cannot start now?"

The earl looked between them. "Now?"

Theodosia ignored him. "Sadly, I have another appointment, or I would stay. Your son does need a lot of work, my lady, so I will ensure we start early, at nine o'clock."

As she placed her notebook back into her reticule, the sofa shifted. The earl had risen and was standing at his full height, evidently attempting to be imposing.

"I would like to say before any more of this nonsense continues," he said in a loud, clear voice, "that I protest. I mean to say, can a man no longer walk the streets of England without being so accosted? Must I fight against such injustice, such cruelty?"

His mother snorted. "Cruelty?"

"I said cruelty, and I meant it," he said fiercely. "I do not want a bride. I do not want a wife. I do not want children running around me. I do not want to make a home with anyone. I did not ask for this, Miss Ashbrooke, and I hope you heed me when I tell you that I intend to make this entire process as difficult as possible!"

His words rang out in the room, and silence followed.

It really was too bad for him.

"Are you quite finished?" she said airily, with a smile. "Wonderful. Always lovely to hear a man attempt to communicate his wishes. Good morning, my lady, so lovely to see you again. My lord, I will see you in your rooms tomorrow, at nine o'clock. I will be punctual. Be prepared."

CHAPTER FOUR

N O MATTER WHAT he tried, Albemarle's fingers just could not stay still. The tassel on the edge of the sofa, a button on his waistcoat—there were no ends of things he could fiddle with while he waited in these godforsaken rooms for the matchmaker from hell.

A clock somewhere in the place struck a quarter to nine, and a dark look swept across his face.

Why in God's name was he doing this? Did he not have his own life, his own routine, his own choices? Had he not plenty of better things to do rather than sitting around waiting for that demon of a woman to turn up and 'train him'?

Albemarle sniffed in disgust in the silence of his drawing room. He could not believe he had agreed to this.

The look his mother had given him flashed through his mind, and he grinned despite himself. *Well, she was a formidable woman.* He did not like crossing her if he could help it.

The damned Ashbrooke woman would be here in ten minutes or so if her protestation at punctuality was correct.

He had given his word, he reminded himself ruefully as he got up to peer out the window. When an earl, your word was important. He could not go back on it now.

Unless...

Unless he simply was not here. An accident, a chance of fate, perhaps, could draw him outside and keep him there until—what, ten o'clock?

Streams of people moved below, the street teeming with people going on their merry way.

No, Albemarle thought darkly. Half tempted as he was to leave his rooms and accidentally miss the irritating woman, he would not take that easy way out.

Besides, Miss Ashbrooke was a little intriguing.

A smile grazed his face as he watched the world go by. His life had not been devoid of strong women, and he was the product of one, after all, and the Greek countryside seemed full of nothing but determined and fierce womenfolk.

But most of those fierce women, whether English or Continental, had been twice his age. They were women who had lived and knew what they wanted, and they were not going to wait around any longer for what they desired.

Miss Ashbrooke was not old. She looked barely five and twenty, despite her serious manner of an older age.

While her peers were simpering, nodding, agreeing with any gentleman who bothered to even look at them—there was Miss Ashbrooke.

Fierce. Irritating. Forceful.

The sound of the doorbell was easily heard by the window, and Albemarle groaned. Ten to nine. She really was punctual.

Footsteps echoed in the passageway, and it was only at that moment he cried out, "Wait before answering the door, Blenkins!"

"Too late, I am afraid, my lord," said Miss Ashbrooke breezily, sweeping into the room and removing her bonnet. "Goodness, what a lovely room. Good morning."

Albemarle leaned against the window frame and attempted to glare, but despite the rising sensation of irritation, he could not help but smile as she removed her pelisse.

Damn Blenkins. He had taken him on from the Earl of Chester, only a footman then. Chester had promised he was a good man, but he needed to be told to listen before opening damn doors.

What did he think he was doing, smiling?

Miss Ashbrooke, despite the removal of her pelisse, was still covered up by her gown buttoned to her neck. Dressed like a woman twice her age, she had taken no care with her hair at all. Just pushed and pinned up, without a second thought. No jewels adorned her ears, her neck, or her fingers.

If he had not known who she was, he would have assumed she was a governess. A housekeeper.

So why was he grinning?

Forcing the smile away, he said gruffly, "Miss Ashbrooke."

She curtseyed and then stood looking at the sofa pointedly without saying a word.

Albemarle smiled. She was in his territory now, and that meant he decided how the game was going to be played. *His rules.*

Without saying a word, he strode past her and threw himself leisurely onto the sofa—without inviting her to sit down. He looked at her, silently.

It was a full minute before she coughed slightly—more a clearing of her throat.

Albemarle could not help but laugh. "Are you so well-mannered, Miss Ashbrooke, that you will not sit down unless you have been invited to?"

Miss Ashbrooke raised an eyebrow. "Are you so ill-mannered, my lord, that you will allow a woman—and a guest—to stand?"

It was delightful. If only they could have met in the Assembly Rooms or at a ball. Sparring with Miss Ashbrooke was the most fun he had had since arriving on this damned, damp island.

What a shame she was attempting to trap him into a marriage he despised.

"I do not know yet," he said aloud. "I think I have made it perfectly clear I have no wish to proceed with this ridiculous charade. I have no desire for a wife, and therefore, no need for your services."

Any other woman would have scowled at his remarks. Some women would have retorted—a small number would have become emotional and upset.

Albemarle was intrigued, he had to admit, to discover which Miss Ashbrooke would choose.

What he did not expect was her to nod. "Yes, I must admit I am gaining little joy from this particular assignment. You forget I am merely a paid subordinate. Your mother has far more influence than I think you care to admit."

As he considered her, he saw she was not the disaster he had assumed. To be sure, Miss Ashbrooke rejected modern fads and fashions, but underneath it all, there was prettiness there.

What his mind had not expected was a vision of what really was underneath. An unconscious smile rose, and he stirred in his seat. *If only half his imagination was correct…*

"My lord? You are drooling."

Albemarle jumped, his hand rushing to his mouth.

Miss Ashbrooke almost laughed. "You were a million miles away, my lord, though I must say whoever had your attention, she must have been pretty."

He coughed. *Allowing his mind to wander was evidently not a clever idea.* "You told me you were a paid subordinate, and so, I will treat you like a servant and speak plainly."

"Please do," she said briskly, still standing. "I will endeavor to do likewise, and—"

Albemarle could not help but laugh. "What, treat me like a servant?"

Finally, a flush of embarrassment colored her cheeks. "No! No, I meant—I meant speak plainly. Do go on, my lord."

There was something delightful about the way she continued to meet his eyes, despite her embarrassment. *Here was a woman who would not back down.*

"Well as I said before, I have no wish for a wife," he said. The sooner this speech finished, the sooner she could leave, and whatever spell Miss Ashbrooke was weaving could be over. "I did this—meet you today, I mean—for my mother's sake, and for that reason only. You can parade as many ladies up and down before me as you like, but that does not mean I will pick one."

What had he expected from this speech? Outrage that he was not interested in matrimony? Concern, perhaps, that he had been hurt before?

None of these followed. Miss Ashbrooke frowned. "Goodness, my lord, what makes you think—"

"Constant effort," he interrupted.

"What makes you think any of them will want to pick you?"

Albemarle had never considered his pride much of a problem. He was an earl, and he acted like one, and therefore he was treated like one. It really was very simple—except with Miss Ashbrooke.

She was starting to remind him of a governess more with each passing moment.

Trying to ignore the prickle to his pride, his voice still sounded a little gruff as he said, "Well damnit, Miss Ashbrooke, I am an earl! I have money, and I am not as ill-featured as—"

"Handsome, I would call it," Miss Ashbrooke interrupted with no sign of embarrassment. "But much to be desired in your manners, I think."

If he thought himself irritated before, he was angry now. *Much to be desired in your manners?*

The cheek of the woman! How dare she come here, ordered by his mother or not, and speak such errant nonsense!

A small, rebellious part of him gloried in her declaration that he was handsome.

Flattered? By a matchmaker?

Was it a coincidence that Miss Ashbrooke looked a little prettier?

"Damned right," he said heavily. "Well, sit down, do. Can't have you floating about the room like a butterfly."

With a rustle of skirts, Miss Ashbrooke stepped around the sofa opposite his own and sat down.

Now she was closer, something strange was happening in his stomach. *Had the eggs Cook did this morning been a little odd?*

"I cannot face arguing with you all day," he said heavily as a horrendous thought struck him. "You—you are not going to be here all day, are you, Miss Ashbrooke?"

"Goodness, I hope not," she said calmly. "I—"

"Because I have many things I wish to do today."

"I am not sure I could stand your company all day."

Albemarle's mouth fell open. *He could not recall ever being spoken to in that ridiculously rude fashion, not ever!*

Miss Ashbrooke was laughing. "My lord, you will find me honest, brutally so, but only because that is usually what people need. The truth is hard to hear, but 'tis even harder to hear if it is buried under niceties, pleasantries, and downright lies."

His mouth was still open, so Albemarle shut it abruptly. He could never have dreamed up such a woman, completely logical, and yet contrary when she wished to be. Teasing him, jesting with him, but from a place of absolute seriousness.

She was, perhaps, unique.

"And now, your training," Miss Ashbrooke said smartly, pulling out her notebook from her reticule. "Genteel conversation, compliments, the growth of a steady temper, reduction of—"

"Do you think all this is necessary?" Albemarle interrupted.

Miss Ashbrooke glared as though he was a dog barking at an inopportune moment. "Reduction of interruptions," she continued, returning to her notebook. "Appropriate conversation topics, appropriate courting behavior, and finally, the proposal."

Albemarle sighed and leaned back into the depths of the sofa. This woman was going to be the death of him. Everything she said and did irritated him beyond belief, and he generally considered himself an easygoing sort of man.

And yet, he could not disagree with her. He did ignore most social conventions around appropriate topics of conversation and never bothered to control his temper nor hide his emotions.

Why should he? He was the fourteenth Earl of Lenskeyn.

She lifted her gaze from her notebook, meeting his own, and something happened. Heat flowed through him, his skin tingled, and every part of his body seemed at once desperate for her touch.

Something was stirring inside him, and he knew exactly what it was. *Desire.*

How like him to be so contrary. Just when he needed to concentrate on escaping this foolish training, his body had decided Miss Ashbrooke was far more delightful as a conquest than as a conversationalist.

So why precisely was Miss Ashbrooke *Miss* Ashbrooke? She was fierce, fiery, and gave as good as she got. She was easy on the eye, too, if one looked past the fashion more suitable for the 1790s.

Albemarle found he was smiling again. Christ, he liked her. If she had been a man, they would probably have been friends.

Forcing down the burgeoning desire, he said, "And which of that terrible list do you suggest we start with?"

Miss Ashbrooke did not seem to have noticed any of his mixed feelings. She was all business, reviewing her list with a careful eye.

"Probably a reduction in interruptions," she said after consideration. "It will make the rest of my training easier to deliver and easier to swallow."

Closing her notebook and restoring it to her reticule, she looked at him critically.

Albemarle shifted uncomfortably. *No one looked at him like that. Why was this woman so damned impertinent?*

"Why do you continuously interrupt people, my lord?"

He blinked. It was not the direction he had expected her to take, and it was a little too deep a question for a quarter past nine in the morning. He usually was not even awake.

"I was not aware I was—"

"Did you start doing it as a child?" Miss Ashbrooke spoke clearly, not raising her voice but allowing it to wash over his own.

Albemarle swallowed. "I think so. You know, I think I did, probably because—"

"And yet, you continue doing it as an adult," she said with a slight frown. "Like many other faults which you have brought into your adulthood."

The flicker of irritation around his heart was growing. "If you would just let me—"

"Nasty habit, you know," said Miss Ashbrooke airily.

His temper, usually frayed and rarely controlled, snapped. "Let me speak, damnit!"

The room went silent, but the matchmaker did not look shocked. Instead, despite all his efforts to the contrary, she was smiling.

"Annoying, is it not?"

Albemarle was breathing heavily but tried to smile.

Damn, she was good. Quicker than most men, quicker than his mother. How had she managed, in just sixty seconds, to demonstrate something no other tutor, mentor, or friend had adequately explained to him?

His fingers had clenched in vexation, but he forced them to relax as his breathing slowed. *If he were not careful, he would find that he had plenty to learn from this Miss Ashbrooke.*

His smile was painfully forced. "Yes, very annoying. Thank you, Miss Ashbrooke."

She nodded, evidently unconcerned with his fury. "Do not concern yourself overly, my lord. 'Tis a common problem for the titled classes, and one which I am slowly breeding out."

Albemarle laughed. "Breeding out?" *The nerve of the woman!*

"Why, yes. I only match gentlemen and ladies on my books who have been cured of this ill. They are the ones who breed. Do you see?"

"God's teeth, woman, but you are terrifying!" He did not bother to self-censor any longer. This woman had no problem being honest, and so he would pay her the same courtesy. "You think you can change the state of the nobility and gentility of England and Ireland with your...your *training*?"

Miss Ashbrooke should have been embarrassed. She should have looked down, colored, and muttered something about her words being but a jest.

She did none of these things. "You cannot argue with the results, my lord. Scores of couples, and quite literally hundreds of children, all raised by parents who, thanks to me, no longer perennially interrupt those around them. I should be knighted."

Albemarle laughed. *She was mad!* She was marvelous. Talking with her was exhilarating.

"You were raised to think your opinion far more interesting than everyone else's," she said calmly. "It is a fault that can be cured, and easily."

He could not help himself. "Really?"

Miss Ashbrooke nodded. "My lord, I am here to tell you that your opinions are utter rot. They are not more interesting than anyone else's—and in fact, I would go so far as to say they are not that interesting at all."

This was too much. In his rooms, a woman paid by his mother to disparage him, and now tell him all he thought, all he believed, was rot?

"You go too far, Miss Ashbrooke," he growled, wanting to get closer to her but fully aware his manhood was doing the thinking. "You have only just met me! You have no comprehension of my opinions."

"I am an excellent judge of character, and I make excellent match-es," she replied swiftly, holding his gaze. "In the eyes of the world, sir,

I have more proof of my intellect than you do of yours!"

Albemarle could not permit this to go any further. This was preposterous. This could not be borne. "I have a degree from Cambridge!"

She did not exactly laugh. No one could call that hastily forced down snort a laugh, but it made Albemarle's spirit wilt.

"Well, yes, your title, you see," she said apologetically, as though explaining the truth of the world to him for the first time. "A title will get you most things. I suppose you have never had to truly try in your whole life."

Albemarle stared at the woman who was rapidly destroying all notions of himself. Not a single person had dared speak to him like that—not since Mr. Lister had spoken damned rudely once at cards.

His fists had seen off that idiot, but the last thing he would ever do was strike a woman. And Miss Ashbrooke did not deserve that. She spoke calmly, as though stating facts. *And her eyes…*

Albemarle could not help but gape. *Could she possibly be right?* Had he gone through life without trouble because everyone else merely stepped out of his way and ensured he got what he wanted?

Was his title, his wealth, that gave him the incredibly comfortable life he enjoyed? Did his name and breeding force everyone to stay quiet when he interrupted them?

Could it be that, actually, he was not good company at all, but merely tolerated?

At the age of nine and thirty, it was a terrible thing to drastically reconsider everything about oneself. Albemarle did not like it, but he could not reject it out of hand. *This would require thinking.*

His gaze refocused. Miss Ashbrooke's smile had not disappeared, but it was softer now. Kinder.

"Good," she said quietly. "You are reevaluating. Everyone must do it at some point, and I would say nearly forty is quite old enough."

Never before had Albemarle felt this vulnerable—and because of a matchmaker! This was intolerable. He could not permit it to continue any longer.

"Are you old enough?" he snapped, frustration and fear pouring into his tones. "When was the last time you had your opinions reevaluated?"

Miss Ashbrooke did not blink. "I perform a self-evaluation every—"

"Oh, well, self-evaluation," Albemarle said with a smile, leaning back and putting his hands behind his head. *He would take back control of this conversation if it were the last thing he did.* "A self-evaluation is easy. 'Tis when other people evaluate you that it gets complicated, and if you ask me, you are a conniving, interfering woman who only makes matches because she cannot get a husband for herself."

Had he gone too far?

"Thank you for your assessment," Miss Ashbrooke said. Was there a coldness in her *words*? "And how do you think you will find a bride with that attitude? Can't you see, my lord, that you need my training and my help if you are ever to be married?"

Albemarle shrugged. This was his territory again now, his breathing calmed, the fire in his lungs dying down. "Money."

The matchmaker sniffed as she closed her notebook. "Money is not everything."

"Surely you cannot believe that, Miss Ashwood. You work for a living!"

"Ashbrooke."

There was a frown on that pretty face now, and it stirred something wicked within him.

"And I choose to work with some of the finest people in the land," she continued, her eyes narrowed. "And that means I do not have to sit here and be insulted!"

Forcing the notebook into her reticule, Miss Ashbrooke rose from her seat and took two steps toward the door. In that instant, a strange rush of pleasure and regret rushed through Albemarle's heart. It was good to finally best her, yes, but he had not imagined she would depart so rapidly. It was amusing, teasing Miss Ashbrooke.

Her hand on the door, she paused and turned, her dark hair illuminated by the sunlight streaming through the window. *It appeared she was taking a deep breath and—surely not counting to ten?*

When Albemarle had reached eight, she smiled. "That is what you want. For me to leave, and for this to be a failure."

He did not reply. He watched her, fascinated. Never before had someone he had driven to their feet stopped to continue speaking to him.

Miss Ashbrooke examined him once again, and the unsettled feeling swept over him. Whenever the matchmaker was looking at him, Albemarle felt...lacking, somehow.

"I do not fail," said Miss Ashbrooke decidedly, removing her hand from the door. "We will have you wed by the end of the season."

"But—"

"You have a title. You cannot be expected to know what good manners are," she said briskly, returning to her seat and arranging her skirts.

Albemarle could not help but watch her delicate fingers at work, mesmerized by the matchmaker who simply would not go away. "We will start from the beginning. A reduction in interruptions. Are you ready?"

CHAPTER FIVE

N O MATTER WHICH direction Robins tugged, Theodosia's reflection was not symmetrical.

"Careful, Robins," she said absentmindedly, feeling a twinge in her shoulder as her neck was pulled. "'Tis only a bonnet."

"I know, Miss Ashbrooke," said the harassed looking maid. "But it just—won't—stay—put!"

Theodosia's shoulder was held steady by one hand as the offending bonnet was shifted left and right. Robins's eyes narrowed in her attempt for perfection.

It was impossible not to smile at the level of concentration, but Theodosia said nothing. *Who was she to complain at a job well done?*

Sometimes she was tempted to go into society with no bonnet whatsoever and allow the breeze to blow through her hair, untamed and unrestricted.

Even the thought of it made her back stiffen. What would people say? She knew what society expected of her—of everyone. It would be most scandalous for her to ignore something as simple as wearing a bonnet in public. *The very idea!*

"Almost there, Miss Ashbrooke," panted the maid, looking as though she was fighting a hideous beast rather than a blue bonnet.

Society had expectations that had to be met. Society was the hideous beast, a ravenous monster that ate people up if they did not conform to its wishes.

She knew better than most the toll that society could take. She had seen it firsthand on those who refused to conform. On those who lied. *On those who were found out.*

Theodosia took a deep breath and forced down the temptation to dwell on him. That was years ago, and she was not going to allow herself to wallow in self-pity.

She had done that far too much. Besides, he did not deserve it.

Smiling at her reflection, she said briskly, "That will do, Robins—and a lovely job you have done of it, I must say. Thank you."

Her maid squinted nervously into the reflection of the looking glass. "Are you certain, Miss Ashbrooke? It is not entirely straight at the back, I am afraid. What if you meet a nice gentleman?"

Theodosia laughed as she turned away. "Well, I almost certainly will not, not today. Even if I do, then he will not be interested in me. I am the matchmaker."

Why did her words pain her? They were the truth, and Theodosia Ashbrooke dealt in harsh realities. If she could not say them to herself, how could she say them to the Earl of Lenskeyn?

"I will be a little late this evening, I am afraid," she said hastily, pushing aside thoughts for the second time in five minutes. "Lady Romeril's card party."

Robins's face fell. "I am so sorry, Miss Ashbrooke. And there is no way around it?"

"'Tis for the best," said Theodosia bracingly. "I have a new gentleman on my books who is determined to challenge me, and it is time I challenged him. Lady Romeril's card parties are always...interesting."

Robins met her gaze, and the two women smiled. Even in polite society, it was possible to refrain from telling the truth, but others would understand.

"The Earl of Lenskeyn cannot hide from me," said Theodosia firmly, placing her hand on the front door.

As she stepped onto the street, a cool breeze hit her face—and the figure of Albemarle Howard, Earl of Lenskeyn, appeared in her path so suddenly, she almost careened into him.

"Mind your—m-my lord!"

Theodosia felt her cheeks color. Mere seconds after her proud pronouncement that she would be in charge of their interactions, here she was, almost toppled to the ground by the mere presence of him!

And what a presence. The earl smiled with that devilishly handsome look she knew could be molded into something quite spectacular.

Not that it needed much improvement.

"I-I thought..." Theodosia swallowed. She needed to regain control of this conversation, for it would not do to lose the high ground. "My lord, the agreement was that we would meet at your rooms, not mine."

He did not immediately reply. The smile remained, and his eyes sparkled as though she had just said something incredibly witty.

Something swooped in Theodosia's stomach, and she forced herself to remain calm. Just a passing fancy. She had noticed the attractive qualities of plenty of her clients before. She would notice them again.

The Earl of Lenskeyn was nothing special.

"I know what we agreed," he said airily, "but I wanted to surprise you. I wished to see if you could be taken by surprise."

Despite Theodosia's internal decision to ignore the man, her heart was beating rapidly as she said brusquely, "Well, of course, you can. Anyone can, given the right conditions. I am not an automaton!"

Why did he stare? They were blocking the pavement, passersby tutting as they were forced to step in the road. And yet, still, he did not move.

"That is what I thought, but I had to be sure," he said, leaning closer. "You are always so composed, so calm. In anyone else, the traits would be irritating."

Theodosia raised an eyebrow and sidestepped him, relieved to be removed from his immediate presence.

"Irritating," she repeated as she started to walk toward his lodgings. "My word."

He fell in step beside her. "You know, I have given much thought to what you said."

Theodosia nodded gracefully at Lady Romeril as they passed, grateful for the presence of the earl, which prevented her from speaking with the older woman. "Which part?"

"All of it."

They had turned a corner now onto Camden Place, where his rooms for the Season were.

She could not help but smile at his blunt response. "That is unusual, and I will admit, not what I had expected. Usually, my words take a lot longer to sink in."

"I told you I was here to surprise you," he said, laughter seeping into his tones. "Did you really think my presence alone was intended to be the surprise?"

He spoke so openly, so unlike the other earls and dukes she had encountered. Theodosia glanced at him and saw his smile had changed once more. No longer calculating, measured, controlled. Now it was open, joyful, almost *teasing*.

A rush of warmth filled her bones as she forced herself to remain calm. She was not here to be impressed by the fourteenth Earl of Lenskeyn. The only reason she was in his presence at all was to train him to become a more suitable consort for a young lady of repute and fortune, then find said young lady.

That was all. She could ignore the rising heat in her body any time she wanted.

"My rooms."

Theodosia jumped. So lost in her thoughts, she had not noticed the earl was now gesturing at number six.

"Thank you," she said stiffly, walking past him up the steps into the building. "How many floors have you taken?"

It took but a few seconds to realize her mistake, and she was grateful for the trail of ribbons at the back of her bonnet, which hid her glowing red neck.

"Floors?" He sounded amused as he followed her inside and pulled off his greatcoat and top hat. "The whole damned place, of course. It's mine."

Theodosia allowed a servant to remove her pelisse, using the time to collect herself. Of course, an earl would not reserve a set of floors in Bath during the Season—the very idea! He would own a whole house in Bath.

Bowing her into the drawing room, the earl waved away his servant without offering her any refreshment. Theodosia opened up her reticule to jot this down in her notebook.

"Sit down, won't you?" He threw himself onto a sofa. "See, I can learn."

She did not permit herself a smile. "Yes, but I still have much to teach. Refreshments, for example. Always offer your guests refreshments, my lord."

He rolled his eyes. "Call me Albie. Everyone does."

Theodosia flushed as she sat opposite him. *Albie?* The very idea she could call him such a name—an earl of the realm, ask his matchmaker to call him Albie?

"I think Lenskeyn is probably the closest I can manage," she said aloud. Even that level of intimacy discomfited her.

In an attempt to distract herself from their strange connection, Theodosia looked around the room.

It was certainly not decorated in his mother's tastes. Number six Camden Place was one of the earl's undoubtedly many homes, and he had fitted it with the latest styles. Curtains mimicking the graceful flow of Grecian columns, the green that had swept Paris and London by storm, were nothing to the delicate paintings on the ceiling depicting cherubs and a few goddesses.

Goddesses with very little clothing.

She had to concentrate. She was here to prepare him for, perhaps, one of the most important social events on the *ton's* calendar.

She would make him ready. Then she would leave. She could not possibly stand another minute in his presence.

"Had your fill?" Lenskeyn's face was mischievous. "Yes, it is all a bit resplendent, but my father would have his way with things. It was a compromise between his taste and my mother's. Anything elegant you see is him. Anything ostentatious is her. And anything like the ceiling..."

His voice trailed away delicately, but the unspoken words were more than enough to cause another rush of heat through Theodosia's body.

She would be mistress of herself. She was the one in charge here, no matter what the title or wealth her clients had.

"Let us return to the matter in hand," she said aloud, as much for her benefit as his.

Lenskeyn rolled his eyes. "Must we? Why is today so important to meet? It was only a few days ago that I had my first foray into gentlemanly behavior, and I am quite exhausted."

"I can imagine."

Her sarcasm seemingly went unnoticed. "My mother said you were quite insistent, and for her to describe anyone in such a way is remarkable."

Ignoring the pointed insult, Theodosia said calmly, "Tonight is Lady Romeril's card party."

"I know," he said heavily. "One of the most prestigious women opening up her house. I almost considered leaving town for a few days when I received the invitation. I had hoped to avoid it."

"Don't we all."

Her comment had been unguarded, breathed rather than spoken, but the room had been so quiet it seemed to echo. *Damn her cheeks, and damn her rebellious tongue!*

"You will need additional training on your charming and courting before we attend this evening," she continued quickly, "which is why we are meeting now, to have sufficient time to practice."

Lenskeyn's brow furrowed as he glanced at the grandfather clock in the corner. "But...Miss Ashbrooke, perhaps you have mistaken the time of the card party's beginning. My invitation indicates we are to arrive at eight o'clock. It is only just gone two o'clock now."

Theodosia nodded. "You need much instruction. Even I am not sure whether we will get through it all."

She spoke calmly, from the heart, and without malice. For some clients, pronouncements of this kind sparked irritation or embarrassment—or even anger.

He laughed. "My dear Miss Ashbrooke, you are tonic to the soul indeed. How do you think I have managed to get through life without being able to charm people?"

"Oh, I don't know," she replied swiftly. "Wealth, a title, connections?"

"Utter rot, and you know it." Lenskeyn scrutinized her with a nonchalant air. "Plenty of titles in the world, plenty of wealth, too. Connections I left behind long ago. You have no need for them in the wilds of Greece. Just the name of the nearest brothel."

Theodosia thought she had done exceptionally well to control her face at that moment. Her instincts–to color, rise to her feet, dramatically storm out, and say she would not be spoken to in this manner–were forced down.

She would be calm. She would show this arrogant, irritating, proud man what she was made of. She would best him.

"If you are going to be difficult," she said sweetly, "we may have to return to respect and politeness."

Their gazes met, hers, as determined as she could make it. His, forceful, yet with some sort of restraint.

What was he not saying?

He raised his hands in surrender, and his voice even had a slightly apologetic tone as he said, "I must say, Miss Ashbrooke—can I call you Theodosia?"

Her heart pounded as she said, "No, you may not."

"I must say, Theodosia," Lenskeyn continued with a mischievous grin, "my mother already says I am much improved in my manners. Who knew not interrupting others could have such an effect! She says you have earned your fee in that mere improvement, even if you do not find me a bride."

She stared. *How would she ever understand this man?* The rudeness of using her name despite her direct refusal of permission, the compliment she was sure had not come from his mother, and the little throwaway ending that aimed to release him from the need to continue training.

He was clever, the Earl of Lenskeyn. But not as smart as her.

"I do not consider the job completed, not just yet," she said briskly. "There is much to improve still."

"Hmm," he pondered. "Perhaps. Do you not think it a little sad that society believes I must be improved—that is to say, forced to be just as average as any other man on the street—before I am to be considered a good marriage prospect?"

Theodosia blinked. The thought had occurred to her about quite a different gentleman, almost two years ago. He had been wild, a little rough around the edges, but he had been endearing.

Society's ladies had not agreed with her. He had come to her desperate to wed, and she had smoothed out all the rough edges of his character.

He had married an heiress three months later. Theodosia had attended the wedding, and she had expected to enjoy it, but there had been something wrong. The gentleman she had met, the one who had endeared himself so, had gone.

The bride seemed happy; the bridegroom seemed ecstatic. Still, none of his friends had attended...

"Ah, I see you agree with me." Lenskeyn leaned forward, his eyes bright. "How fascinating. A matchmaker who preaches to the world's gentlemen that they must be one way, but who secretly believes it should be the other."

Theodosia swallowed. *This had gone on long enough.* "Gentlemen are not the only ones who are encouraged to grow in maturity and wisdom—so do society's ladies, and I can assure you that my training is offered to both the sexes. Now, charming and courting."

Whatever response she had expected, it was not the one she received. Lenskeyn tilted over, falling onto the sofa with his eyes shut, loud snores emanating from his nose.

Theodosia rolled her eyes. *Just when she thought she was getting somewhere...*

"My lord," she said, and then a little louder, "Lenskeyn!"

Neither of these pronouncements seemed to be getting her anywhere. Much against her better nature, she leaned forward and prodded him.

Lenskeyn sat up quickly and looked around wildly. "Is it over?"

She would not give in. "Why are you not trying? You are more child than man today, my lord, and I tell you straight, I am tired of it!"

"As am I." He glared, leaning closer once again. "This whole matchmaking business, you know, I had no wish to partake in this nonsense in the first place. I do not want to be introduced to a slip of a thing who has barely left the nursery! I want you."

It took a moment for the words to register, but then Theodosia reacted the only way she knew. She laughed.

What a ridiculous thing to say—what a wild joke!

"Please, Lenskeyn, be serious," she said, still smiling. "We have much to go through in the topics of charming and courting."

She had thought he would join in with her laughter after making such a ridiculous pronouncement. But the earl was looking at her carefully, examining her features.

"Is it so strange to think a gentleman would be interested in you?" he spoke quietly, but for the first time that day, with sincerity. "So strange you would laugh?"

Theodosia shook her head. "Now, really, Lenskeyn, I admit you are clever with a joke, but we need to push on. Now, when it comes to charming—"

"I know you have instructed me not to interrupt, but I cannot help it." Each word was chosen with care, and that earnest look had not disappeared. "Theodosia, and I will keep calling you Theodosia, because it is a pretty name, and you are quite pretty. And fierce. By God, I like you."

She stared, flickers of confusion racing through her heart as her entire body felt as though electricity had been forced through it.

He was jesting, of course. But there was no look of jollity on his face, those handsome lines still in the position of complete sincerity.

"Y-You cannot mean that," she said aloud, hating how foolish her words sounded.

The Earl of Lenskeyn, her client, consider *her* pretty? Every inch shivered at the very thought.

"Fierce and pretty," he said, his handsome face creasing into a grin. "Damn woman, I never thought I would say this, but I like you. Yes, I will have *you*."

Theodosia could hear her pulse. "You will have me?"

Lenskeyn nodded with a look of total satisfaction. "Yes. Well, if I have to marry, and I can see why Mother makes such a fuss of it now Elmore is gone, God rest his soul, why not marry someone I can bear to speak to for more than five minutes at a time?"

He appeared to be in earnest. The thought shocked her—the shock quickly followed by panic and then a strange desire to laugh.

This cannot be happening. Not again.

"B-But I—you cannot..." Theodosia swallowed, tasting the panic in her throat and breathing in deeply. *She would not lose control.* "You simply cannot mean that, my lord. I am here to find you a match, for that is what a matchmaker does. It would be most improper for the matchmaker to get married!"

What she did not say, because she would not lie, was that she did not wish to marry him.

The very idea was ridiculous, and she would only entertain it here, in the solitude of her thoughts.

But...*well*. He was a handsome man, and she was certain she could tame him. Albie Howard, the dashing gentleman who paid no heed to the rules and little heed to society. To be free of expectations, of work, of daily counting her carefully saved pounds. What a wild life she could lead as the Countess of Lenskeyn.

Before she had another chance to speak, Albie—the earl, she hastily corrected herself—had risen and was now seated beside her.

Heat rushed through her body, and her fingers twisted in her lap.

So close.

"You have never thought," he said in a low voice, "of making a match for yourself?"

Theodosia swallowed. *Had he noticed her response to him?* Had she been so unguarded in her...admiration, not attraction, that he had noticed?

"No, of course not," she said hurriedly, avoiding his gaze. "That would be most indecorous."

Albie had taken her hand in his and held it tightly. The skin to skin contact was intoxicating.

"Theodosia, you are missing something precious. Something delicious. Something I would happily—"

"My lord, you are most playful today," she managed to say as she pulled her hand from his. "I think we should—"

"Call me Albie."

Theodosia gave in to temptation. She tilted her head and looked into his eyes.

From that instant, she was utterly transfixed. *How could she look away?* There was something intoxicating about him. Wild, yet tamed. Rude, and yet the arrogance was not selfish. *Bold.* So sure of himself that he would say anything, do anything, be anywhere he wanted.

Her hands were somehow in his again. "Do not be ridiculous, Lenskeyn."

He raised an eyebrow. His warmth was radiating into her, his hands encircling hers in a way that was…that made her feel…

"Albie…" she whispered. It felt right. The fear of intimacy was gone—how could it stay, her hands in his, with her eyes locked into his own?

Saying his name felt rebellious and extraordinary. She wanted to repeat it, but she would not. *She had to stop this. This had gone on long enough.*

"Your games are not going to work on me," Theodosia breathed.

He smiled wickedly. "Really?"

His lips met hers before she knew what was happening, and while Miss Ashbrooke, matchmaker, knew she should push him away, Theodosia would call him Albie until the end of her days.

It was exquisite. It was wonderful. He was passionate yet respectful, worshiping her with his mouth as she melted into him, unable to prevent her body's response.

Perhaps it was time to throw caution to the wind. His hands released hers, but only to pull her closer, and Theodosia found her hands, now free, were able to push him away.

They did not. Instead, inexplicably, they found themselves tangled in that wild mane of hair, pulling him closer as her lips parted, and his tongue started to tease her own.

She had not been kissed like this since—well, she had never been kissed quite like this. Albemarle was everything in that moment, everything in the world. This moment could never end.

"You have never thought of making a match for yourself?"

Could his offer have been in earnest? Could she engage herself to a client?

The thought was enough to break the kiss finally. Pulling away from him and standing, she coughed and smoothed down her gown.

"Very—very good, my lord, I can see you were right."

She allowed herself a glance and saw with just a hint of pride, he looked dazed.

"I am right?"

Theodosia nodded. She had to keep talking—anything to slow the frantically beating heart that was threatening to burst from her chest.

"You do not need training in charming and courting after all," she said, picking up her reticule and ensuring her notebook was inside. *Anything to avoid his gaze.* "I will see you at Lady Romeril's card party this evening, eight o'clock prompt, so you can continue to practice your new skills."

She had almost reached the door to the hallway before Albie had risen to his feet.

"Now, wait a moment!"

"I am sorry, I have another appointment," Theodosia lied hurriedly.

"Another appointment be damned," he said fiercely, reaching for her. "I would rather practice kissing now, here, with you."

Despite her desire to be touched by him again, kissed by him, pulled into his arms, Theodosia's instincts were stronger. *She would not allow herself to fall down into this trap again.*

He was only teasing, after all. No earl would seriously consider her as a marriage prospect. She knew that now.

"I think you are teasing me," she said aloud, "and attempting to irritate your Mother. Eight o'clock, my lord."

She only just managed to leave the drawing room—but within a minute, Theodosia was halfway down the street with her pelisse over one arm and a confused heart frantically beating.

CHAPTER SIX

L AUGHTER ECHOED AROUND the room, carried by the smoke rising from cigars. The sound of coins hitting the tables and giggles from ladies rose above them all.

Lady Romeril always hosted the best parties, yet she was a difficult woman at times. There was a reason that her invitations were coveted by all in society. Punch and wine flowed, there was merriment everywhere one looked, and Albemarle was bored to tears.

"Fold," he said listlessly, placing his hand onto the table.

"Why, my lord, what an interesting choice!" Miss Lymington's voice grated on his nerves, and she giggled. "Why, you did not even look at them."

Albemarle shrugged without answering. *What did it matter?* He had not come here for Lady Romeril's approval, nor to be seen by society's greats, nor to win at cards.

He had only come to the damn card party because Theodosia was supposed to be here.

He almost laughed. Attending one of society's most important events in the first place was a strange one for him. There had been nothing like this in Greece. Even his brief visits to Paris had not been like this. All feathers and fans, hoping to attract, preening, and shoving.

It turned his stomach. This was precisely the reason he had left Bath, left England, in the first place.

He had only been thirty minutes late.

"I will see you at Lady Romeril's card party this evening, eight o'clock

prompt, so you can continue to practice your new skills."

A smile unconsciously crept across his face. Well, he had done his best, but almost forty years of bad habits could not be entirely undone in mere days.

Still, he was here, and she was not. It was almost half-past nine now, if he could make out the clock on the other side of the room clearly. Had he missed her? Had she arrived at eight and left after seeing he was not here?

"Well, how intriguing," Miss Lymington simpered.

Pretty, in a way, and an heiress, he had heard. He was sure Theodosia would consider her an excellent match for him.

But she simply could not compare to the real thing. *To Theodosia.*

His whole body shivered as he recalled the impetuous kiss he had stolen just hours before.

"Come on then, Miss Lymington, play your cards," Viscount Braedon said with a grin. "Leave the stuffy old man to his thoughts."

Albemarle did not take offense at the jest. He did want to be left alone with his thoughts, with the memory of Theodosia Ashbrooke in his arms.

God, but she had been sweet. He had only intended to tease her—at least, at first—something to entertain and to distract from the boredom of her ridiculous training.

The teasing had ceased the moment his lips had touched hers.

In that instant, Albemarle had thrown aside all thoughts of teasing this determined woman and instead embraced her as she needed. As she deserved. As he wanted.

He had kissed plenty of misses in his time, all over Europe. He was no stranger to the first kiss, the way one's body yearned for another's, and the sweet release of tension as lips finally met.

This had been different. *Theodosia had been different.*

He was here, as Theodosia—his matchmaker—had demanded. *So, where was she?*

"And that's the hand that wins the spoils!" Braedon threw down his cards and laughed as the rest of the table groaned. "Now, what did I tell you? I never bluff—if I raise, then 'tis because I have the cards. Come on, pay up, Wynn."

Viscount Wynn was not going to consent without grumbling. "I still do not understand how the cards continue to favor you."

Braedon shrugged with a mischievous grin. "Do not blame me, blame Lady Luck! Goodness, you look serious, Lenskeyn. What are you thinking about?"

Albemarle smiled but was unable to answer before Miss Lymington leaned forward eagerly. "I think he is waiting for someone!"

She smiled coquettishly, her eyelashes fluttering.

He smiled mechanically. "And why do you say that, Miss Lymington?"

"Why, 'tis obvious!" She fluttered her fan now that her cards were played, her eyes fixed on his own. "You keep looking at the door, my lord, and you have spared nary a moment of your concentration on the game. Who is she?"

Damn and blast it. The woman was not just full of hot air. She had been watching him for some time.

Miss Darby, the fifth at their table, had wide eyes. A pleasant enough girl, Albemarle had thought within moments of meeting her, but not bright.

"Everyone in Bath seems to be here," Braedon said, pulling the cards toward him and starting to shuffle the deck. "The Duke of Axwick is not here, although I suppose that is to be expected."

"I had hoped to meet the Earl of Marnmouth finally," said Wynn ruefully. "I thought he would be here."

Braedon snorted as he dealt the next hand. "Old Marnmouth has gone into hiding, now that he and Miss Tilbury have parted ways…"

Albemarle smiled. Braedon could not help but follow the gossip whenever it touched Miss Emma Tilbury, the former mistress of Marnmouth. There had been talk that they would reconcile, but that had passed into nothing.

"—thought Miss Ashbrooke would be here, too," Wynn said as he looked irritably at his cards.

He must control himself. He must keep his interest in the woman under wraps.

It would never do to start a rumor of his own.

"Oh?" he said as casually as he could manage. "The matchmaker?"

Wynn nodded as Miss Darby made her first bet. "Yes, the very one. You know, I heard she was wrapped up in the Orrinshire and Seton business. You must have heard about it, even from the depths of the Continent. From what I heard, he practically jilted his first engagement."

There was a gasp from Miss Darby and a tut from Miss Lymington.

Well, really. Albemarle tried not to roll his eyes as he looked at his cards. Two kings and a nine. Ladies did make a mountain out of a molehill. *So the man did not wish to marry someone?* He could hardly blame him.

"I heard much the same thing," said Miss Lymington in a whisper designed to encourage him to lean closer. He did no such thing. "It was a wonder the scandal was hushed up. Miss Ashbrooke did well there."

Despite his indifference toward her, Miss Lymington had now finally piqued Albemarle's interest.

"Oh, you know her, then?"

Miss Lymington laughed as Miss Darby said earnestly, "Oh, yes, everyone knows Miss Ashbrooke."

"And everyone has a story to tell about her," Miss Lymington interjected with a grin.

Albemarle smiled mechanically. It was too bad he outranked poor Braedon, who looked like he could do with a little flattery from Miss Lymington.

"Indeed," he said, placing down his bet. "And have you been desperate enough to pay for her services then, Miss Lymington?"

It was a rather callous remark, he would admit, but it washed over Miss Lymington like water off a duck's back.

"Oh, no, I am fortunate enough not to require Miss Ashbrooke's services," she purred. "And yet, I will admit, for many, it is not desperation. It is in search of true love."

Braedon snorted. "True love?"

"You do not believe in such a thing?" Wynn asked, peering at his cards with a shake of his head.

Albemarle shot a warning look at Braedon, but he was too immersed in his cards to notice.

"I am not saying good matches do not happen," he said, ignoring the growing irritation on his companion's face. "I am just saying I do not believe in true love, that there is merely one person you can experience the joys of life with."

Albemarle could see an argument was about to break out between Braedon, the blustering, well-meaning fool that he was, and Wynn, who from memory had recently married.

He was not the only one to notice.

"Oh, is it my turn?" Miss Darby said more loudly than strictly necessary. "Yes, Miss Ashbrooke is marvelously talented. She can find anyone a partner."

"I think I will fold," Miss Lymington said, leaning to place the cards on the table and allowing Albemarle rather more view of her breasts than was strictly acceptable in public. "I am surprised you have not heard of her prowess before, my lord. My sister—my twin sister, Isabella, you know—was matched by Miss Ashbrooke only last year. They marry in a few months and, by all accounts, will be very happy. 'Tis a long engagement, I suppose."

Intrigue rose in his heart. Theodosia had an excellent reputation. *A perfect match, one's true love, someone ideally suited...*

It did not seem possible, and yet time and time again, she had done it.

"How?" he asked.

Miss Lymington, evidently glorying in his attention, shrugged. The movement made the diamonds around her neck catch the candlelight, and Albemarle could not help but glance down at the way they nestled into her breasts.

"How would I know?" she said with a smile. "She is the matchmaker. She makes it happen."

Wynn laughed as he raised the stakes. "Come on now, Lenskeyn, you know better than that. Do not ask a magician how they perform their tricks!"

"I think it incredible how she manages it," said Braedon, brow furrowed as he concentrated on their game. "So many people never find a partner at all, and yet she manages to not only encourage people to get married but stay married!"

Albemarle glanced at Miss Darby. She was the quietest at their table, quite unlike what Braedon had warned him about. She was known, apparently, for her chattering nature.

He had thought at first she was devoted to Braedon. Now, however, he saw her look just beyond the viscount's shoulder.

A tall, dark, and miserable looking man was standing across the room. He looked over to their table, and Miss Darby looked away quickly, her cheeks reddening.

"You remember Miss Coulson?"

Everyone around the table laughed, even Miss Darby.

"Sorry, was I supposed to laugh?" Albemarle said, irritation seeping into his voice. Just another reason why he had left this damned country. So many jokes that one had to know to join into polite society.

"Apologies, old thing," Braedon said with a good-natured grin as he raised in the final round. "But it was so talked about across Bath and London, I assumed you heard."

"I have not been in society much, if at all," Albemarle retorted, trying to keep his irritation down. "Who is this Miss Coulson, and what has she done to elicit such laughter from you all?"

"We should not laugh, really," said Miss Lymington hurriedly. "There is no harm in her, and she is a delightful thing, but...well. Her topics of conversation are rather limited."

"Rather limited?" Wynn grinned as he displayed his hand—a full house, which made the table groan. "Come on now, everyone, 'tis just a game, no need to be so sore."

"Limited?" Albemarle prompted. He could not think why he was interested in this poor woman's story, but any connection to Theodosia and his spirits picked up.

"I would say so. Sewing, embroidery, that sort of thing," Miss Lymington said dismissively. "My word, but she was dull. I was seated beside her at Lady Howard's, once, and I tell you, I almost cried at the boredom of it all."

"So many people thought," said Miss Darby, looking a little abashed. "We shouldn't laugh, really, but her parents grew concerned that she would never find a match. Her parents scraped together and found the fee for Miss Ashbrooke. Five weeks later, she was engaged to a tailor."

Albemarle frowned. *A tailor? A tradesman?*

"Lenskeyn is not impressed," said Braedon with a grin. "Yes, well, may you look down on such a trade, but not everyone has titles and wealth pouring from their ears. Mr. Weston is a well-respected tailor to the nobility and St. James' Court, and you have probably worn some of his creations, though you may not have known it."

"An excellent match for her, and by all accounts, Mrs. Weston is pleased," said Miss Lymington drily, making it clear no tailor would do for her.

"You know, I find that rather impressive," Albemarle admitted. "She had been ignored, cast aside by society—and many of you, by the sounds of it—and Theo…Miss Ashbrooke, I mean, was able to turn her peculiarity into a success."

Braedon pulled a cigar from his waistcoat along with his tinderbox. "Yes, I suppose it was rather impressive. She's not good company, though."

Albemarle started at the strange comment as his companion lit his cigar. "Not good company?"

"The trouble is, whenever in her presence, you just know you are …well, sized up," said Wynn almost apologetically as he rearranged his stacks of coins. "Before I met Letitia, I avoided her."

"Difficult, though, when she attends every blasted wedding," muttered Braedon as he pulled on his cigar. "Oh, apologies, ladies."

Miss Darby was too busy attempting to catch the eye of the gentleman on the other side of the room, and Miss Lymington merely simpered.

Albemarle rolled his eyes. "Strange, I found her quite interesting."

"Yes, but she is not short of gentleman at the moment, so I have heard," Braedon said with a laugh. "Short on ladies! Always on the hunt for an eligible young lady to add to her roster, so that when the right gentleman comes along…"

The table laughed as Wynn started to deal the next hand.

"I did not know your sister had used Miss Ashbrooke's services," he said as he passed her a card. "How did that come about?"

Miss Lymington smiled and started to tell the story, which to Albemarle's mind sounded rather dull and nothing like the Miss Ashbrooke he had encountered.

No, Theodosia was utterly different. When he had taken her hands into his own, he had felt…something he had never felt before.

The sensation of her lips on his own…and she had not pulled away. Quite the opposite. His neck prickled as he remembered the sensation of her hands pulling him closer.

He had seen the desire in her eyes when she had risen to escape.

She wanted more. She had tasted carnality and wanted it—but refused. The cast-iron grip on herself had slipped, but only for a moment.

How much more pleasure could he take from her? How much could he give?

"Ah, I see what has happened."

Braedon's voice cut into his thoughts, and he looked conspiratorially at the table.

"What has happened?" Miss Darby looked a little flustered.

Braedon grinned. "You have decided to contract Miss Ashbrooke to find you a wife, have you not, you old dog?"

Albemarle sighed. *What was the point in lying?* "My mother has."

Wynn almost sprayed his wine across the green baize, and Miss Lymington shifted her chair closer to Albemarle.

"You can laugh," he said to Wynn in particular and the table in general, "but if your accounts are correct, you never know. She might find my true love!"

Braedon grinned. "Maybe."

"Maybe," Miss Lymington said softly under the noise of the room, "you have already met her."

Albemarle was not stupid. He was not ignorant of the ways young ladies attempted to catch future husbands, and Miss Lymington was perhaps the most blatant of the lot.

She was pretty, to be sure. *But she was not Theodosia.* It was a foolish thought, but one he could not help.

He inclined his head gracefully without saying anything.

Then he blinked. *Damned teeth, why did he not say something cutting?* An insult, something to put Miss Lymington and her heaving breasts in her place.

Just a week ago, that would have been precisely what he would have done. Today, he left it at that.

Was Miss Theodosia Ashbrooke having such an effect on him already?

"Well, you will soon be able to tell us whether Miss Ashbrooke is as impressive as rumor would have us believe," said Miss Darby with a small smile. "Unless she has found someone for you already?"

Albemarle laughed. "No, I do not think it will be possible for her to find—"

"There you are, my lord."

A hand had fallen firmly onto his shoulder, and as Albemarle turned around to see who had so rudely interrupted him, his mouth fell open.

Theodosia.

"You do not mind if I borrow him, do you, my lords, Miss Lymington, Miss Darby?"

She was smiling at his table companions. *Was she avoiding his eyes?* Albemarle swallowed and found his throat dry. He rose hastily to his feet, his chair falling in his haste, and he smiled idiotically.

"Oh dear," she said with no recognition in her eyes that just a few hours ago, she had been in his arms being thoroughly kissed. "We may have to consider some additional conversations about spatial awareness, my lord. Now, come and meet Miss Worsley."

Albemarle's face fell. For an instant, he had forgotten the reason they had met here in the first place.

He could see out of the corner of his eye that Braedon and Wynn were carefully keeping their faces neutral, but they could have taken a leaf from Theodosia's book. She was looking at him as though they had only met but a handful of times—which, now he thought about it, was true.

She was going through with it then, just as his mother had instructed her. *A bride for the earl! What nonsense.*

"Come on, my lord," she repeated as though speaking to a child who did not wish to attend school. "Miss Worsley is waiting."

Albemarle stepped around the fallen chair without saying a word. As soon as he could explain he had no interest at all in speaking with Miss Worsley, whoever she—

"Ah, Miss Worsley, there you are."

Albemarle found he was now standing before a young woman who looked just as bored and disinterested as he felt.

She curtseyed, however, and as he bowed, she said, "It is an honor to make your acquaintance, my lord."

"The pleasure is all mine," Albemarle rushed through before immediately turning away. "Theodosia—Miss Ashbrooke, I wished to speak with you about—"

For a woman who had attempted to train him out of the habit of interruptions, she was a most infuriating woman.

"Not now, my lord," Theodosia said airily with a swift smile that disappeared as quickly as it arrived. "I need to speak with Lady Wynn, but I leave you in the capable hands of Miss Worsley."

She had bustled off before she had reached the end of her sentence, leaving him standing in silence with Miss Worsley. The entire occupants of his card table were goggling. Albemarle felt a flush threaten to blossom out from his cravat. *This was intolerable!*

"You look a little discomforted from being seated so long, my lord," said Miss Worsley graciously.

"'Tis nothing, I assure you," he said quickly. Theodosia was on the other side of the room, speaking with a woman who looked incredibly shy. "Will you take a turn about the room with me?"

She inclined her head in agreement but did not reach for his arm. *Thank goodness*, Albemarle thought hazily, *or I would have been obliged to take it. Who knows what the gossips of the ton would have thought about that?*

"Are you enjoying Bath?"

Ironically, the only woman he wished to be joined with in a rumor was the reason he was stuck with this Miss Worsley. Albemarle kept his eyes on Theodosia as she elegantly made her way around the room. She was a natural—never staying too long, but always leaving her conversationalists with a smile.

"I said, are you enjoying Bath?"

A flicker of jealousy curled around Albemarle's heart as Theodosia placed her hand on a gentleman's arm. *How dare she just flaunt herself like that, knowing he wished to speak with her?*

"My lord!" Miss Worsley's voice was sharp.

He blinked. "What?"

"I said, how are you enjoying Bath?" Her face was a picture of annoyance, but she controlled herself and tried to smile.

Poor woman. Raised in the same poisonous society he knew all too well. He could be her best possible opportunity for a match. *What a strange world they lived in.*

"Oh, you know," he said with a shrug.

Miss Worsley expected there to be more, but when the silence had continued for another minute as they walked around the room, she tried again.

"I have not seen you in town before, I think, nor Bath."

"No," he said shortly. "I am not often here."

Now, where was she? Ah, yes, speaking with Lady Romeril. Goodness, Theodosia had the patience of a saint to spend more than a minute with that woman.

"I am in Bath quite often," said Miss Worsley with no spirit in her words.

Albemarle sighed. It was quite possible for him to have a charming, nay, sparkling conversation with Miss Worsley. He would amaze her, impress her with his wits, make her laugh, make her feel important, special.

But he would rather speak with Theodosia. His damned matchmaker. What was happening to him?

"You will have to excuse me, Miss Worsley," he said without a second glance as he moved toward Theodosia.

"Well, really!"

He was too far across the room to bother replying, even if he had wanted to. "Theodosia."

She was speaking now to an elderly couple, but she had no opportunity to make polite goodbyes to them. That was because Albemarle had taken her by the arm and pulled her across the room, through the door, and into the hallway.

"Albemarle Howard, that was very rude!"

"I do not care," he said roughly, dropping her arm and moving closer to her. He wanted to be closer to her. *He needed to be.* "Miss Worsley is boring."

Theodosia stared. "Miss Worsley is a well-known wit!"

"I would rather talk to you." He did not care how many other people were moving along the hallway into different rooms, looking for friends, avoiding enemies. Smoke and the sound of laughter made the whole place feel hazy.

Theodosia rolled her eyes. "This nonsense again—come here, let me show you something."

Enthralled, Albemarle allowed himself to be pulled into a different room. *What could she have to show him? Was it, perhaps, a ruse to get him alone so she could speak with him privately?*

"Good evening, Miss Marnion," said Theodosia with a smile as she stopped before a lady with the most extravagant feathers in her hair that he had ever seen. "Albemarle Howard, Earl of Lenskeyn. Miss Agatha Marnion."

Albemarle could have shouted with frustration. *Another young lady dangled under his nose!*

"I actually meant—pleasure to meet you, Miss Marnion—Theodosia, I wanted—"

"The earl and I were just discussing Mozart," Theodosia said breezily to the woman who had pinked at being introduced to an earl. "But then, I think sometimes Salieri is to be preferred. What do you think, Miss Marnion?"

"I—well, I have many thoughts on this subject," she said in surprise, eyes darting between Theodosia and Albemarle.

The matchmaker smiled. "Really? What a coincidence. Miss Marnion is a budding musician and greatly enjoys chamber music," she said to him as she walked away.

He stared, open-mouthed, at the audacity of the woman.

"Although Mozart is perhaps better known, I do believe Salieri has many superior compositions," Miss Marnion said, a little timidly. "What do you think, my lord?"

His mouth was still open, but no words came.

After all his posturing, his sharp words to his mother, his jest with Theodosia—it had come true.

He liked her. Of all the ladies he had ever met, it was his damned matchmaker who had caught his eye.

Her spark. Her fire. Her determination to ignore him when it suited.

She was his match, there was no doubt about it. All this standing around and being introduced to other ladies was a fool's errand when he had already found the woman he wished to bed and wed.

CHAPTER SEVEN

A GAGGLE OF ladies walked by Theodosia as she settled onto a bench in Sydney Gardens. The sun was bright, dancing off their jewelry, and she could not help but smile. Their laughter, albeit at a distance and naught to do with her, was infectious.

Unlike the first group, which had appeared a little too old to be suitable, this group contained two or three ladies who would have been perfect matches for a few of her gentlemen.

If she had not agreed to meet the Earl of Lenskeyn at this particular bench, she would have raced after them. One could never be too eager to sign a few more pretty girls onto the books, especially when so short of them.

If the earl arrived on time, she would have been able to explain to him what she needed to do and spoken with them.

As it was...

The women turned the corner and disappeared. Theodosia sighed heavily and glanced at the church tower on the other side of the gardens. It clearly showed twenty minutes past three.

Irritation flared, but it was tempered by her racing heart as Albemarle crossed her mind.

She had woken not once but thrice last night from dreams in which she had not managed to reach the drawing room door almost a week ago.

No, in her dreams, he had slammed the door closed and pulled her into his arms.

They had been heady, untamed dreams. Dreams that made her question whether she had made the right decision in the moment.

The same feelings were stirred when she had arrived ten minutes early for their three o'clock appointment today. She had wanted to see him, longed for it, despite having seen him the day before.

A day without him was starting to feel meaningless.

Theodosia shook herself. She should not have kissed him—or at least, she should not have permitted him to kiss her. That was where all this trouble had started.

She was the matchmaker. She was supposed to be finding him a wife!

The trouble was, despite her best efforts—efforts at odds with her spirit, as her soul hated seeing him with any other lady—the Earl of Lenskeyn was no closer to the wedding aisle than when she had first started.

In the last week, she had introduced him to no fewer than six of her best ladies, and that did not include the serendipitous introductions to ladies such as Miss Marnion.

Theodosia smiled as she watched a boy play with his dog, his parents looking on fondly. Poor Miss Marnion. She had not deserved to have Albemarle thrust upon her like that, and in public, too.

She had almost forgone attendance at Lady Romeril's card party. Anything to avoid him and the way he made her feel.

But her absence would have gained far more comment than her attendance, and so she had attempted to palm him off—first to Miss Worsley, who had been strangely demure that evening, and then to Miss Marnion.

Whether Albemarle found someone to enjoy the evening with, she did not know. She had left before her self-control deserted her, and she permitted him to kiss her again.

Theodosia watched the dog fetch a stick for the boy who shouted something back to his parents, seated on a similar bench to hers. A pair of ladies, arm in arm, walked past her, chattering about some delectable bit of gossip one of them had just heard.

"That is what I said!"

"Well, you had guessed her affections were otherwise engaged when you saw them at…"

Theodosia watched them with the eye of an expert. Too flighty to be seriously desiring a match, too young to be considering marriage at this stage. Too silly to be a good match for Lenskeyn.

What was it he had said about one of the ladies she had introduced him to?

"Far more interested in spending my money than holding the hand that offered it."

She smiled. He did have a way with words, and a cutting remark from him would hurt to the core. She would not want to be on the receiving end.

"Theodosia, if you make me marry that one, I shall have to hire you as a nanny. She's a complete child."

She laughed aloud, gaining a few intrigued looks from those walking in Sydney Gardens. Forcing a more solemn expression, she scolded herself silently.

One cannot just sit on a bench in public and laugh randomly! She was supposed to be giving the Earl of Lenskeyn another lesson today. At least, she would be, as soon as he decided to arrive.

She must not get distracted. She must stop thinking about the way she would tease him, the words she would use to tempt him, and how she would step away from him to drive him even wilder.

But the earl in her mind's eye did not take kindly to being treated in that way. No, he followed her, pinning her against a convenient wall, kissing her neck so tenderly that she…

Theodosia coughed. *It was most improper to have such thoughts. Ladies did not obsess over these sorts of things. If Albemarle ever knew how much she daydreamed about him…*

She swallowed. He never could. She would never permit herself the wild abandon that it would take for her to reveal such nonsense. She needed to be serious.

She needed to find him a bride as quickly as possible.

Pulling her reticule onto her lap, she pulled out her notebook and started writing on a fresh new page.

E. of Lenskeyn unimpressed with all introductions to date. Primary concerns: age (too young), temperament (too flighty), and interest in wealth not person.

When she had first encountered him, she would have laid money on Albemarle being happy with a pretty young thing on his arm, as long as he did not have to spend too much time with her.

But he was more introspective than that. More desirous of someone he could respect. And yet, when she had introduced him to someone quite perfect, he had turned his nose up—quite literally.

It had been a miracle of her matchmaking skills that Miss Jones had not taken real offense. She would now have to make a better introduction for Miss Jones to assuage her irritation.

L. not committed to matrimony; all signs point toward lethargy.

Not committed to matrimony in the slightest. At least, not to anyone she had presented to him.

L. not interested in training, disrupts all attempts at improvement.

She could not help but smile. No, he certainly had no interest in changing or improving, even for her. He had not wished for matrimony in the first place, and he had vehemently argued against a matchmaker.

Improving. Theodosia had never met a gentleman who could not benefit from a few tweaks to his personality, and in all cases, these had led to much greater success in courting.

Even a few ladies, now she considered it, had accepted a few delicately made comments about their person or personality, which had aided them in the pursuit of a suitor.

Consider Miss Coulson. If Theodosia had not managed to find Mr. Weston, she would have had to make quite drastic changes.

The wind picked up, pulling at the pages of her notebook.

Albemarle was different. True, he sorely needed improvement. His mother had described him as a real challenge, what felt like weeks ago at the Orrinshire wedding, and she had not been wrong. But he had not changed a whit since they had met, and yet she liked him more than ever.

He was rude, but seen in a different light, that characteristic was just honesty. He spoke his mind. One always knew where they stood with the Earl of Lenskeyn.

He was arrogant, but that came from a knowledge of himself. He was clever, well-educated, and well-traveled. He was wealthy and had a title. It was surely impossible not to be arrogant with that lineage.

He had almost stopped interrupting her, but as it was usually with a witty remark or something that made her smile, she never let that bother her. Besides, she just interrupted him back.

It was rare to find a gentleman whose company she found interesting, and the novelty had not worn off.

Most of the pups she found wives for were, if she was frank, boring. That was the skill of a matchmaker, finding something of interest within a person and drawing it out to ensure they could attract a partner.

The earl had the opposite problem. He was all attractiveness. Everything about him drew her closer.

What she did not understand was why so few ladies felt the same magnetism.

The family nearby had moved on, the dog unable to drag home the heavy stick it had found. A large family, seven children at least, were now playing on the lawn.

"I would rather practice kissing now, here, with you."

Theodosia's cheeks burned. It was all nonsense, this obsession, this crush she had developed for her most eligible gentleman.

Almost as nonsensical as his strange declaration, all those nights ago.

"I do not want to be introduced to a slip of a thing who has barely left the nursery! I want you."

Theodosia gripped her notebook. Albemarle had just been teasing her; there was no other explanation for it.

After all, no one wished to marry the matchmaker. She was never the bride. It was always someone else's story that she was merely a part of—an instrumental role, to be sure—but not the heroine.

The church clock chimed half-past three. Theodosia sighed heavily and placed her notebook back into her reticule. This was the first time the earl had failed to meet with her when arranged, and she could not help but feel despondent. A day without him seemed so gray, so empty.

"Shame," said a voice behind her. "I was hoping to see what you had written about me."

Theodosia whirled around to see Albemarle smiling.

"You thought I wasn't coming? Nonsense, I'm just fashionably late."

Before she could say anything, he had walked around the bench and kissed her hand, making her heart flutter. *She must not allow herself this weakness. She must be strong.*

The last thing she needed was the ever-perceptive earl to notice how she felt about him.

"You," she said instead, frowning, "are very late."

Albemarle threw himself on to the bench in the manner she had quickly grown accustomed to and smiled. "Nonsense. You are early. You cannot possibly know if I am late. Do you have a pocket watch on you?"

Theodosia pointed at the large clock atop the church tower. It showed twenty minutes to four.

"It is slow," he said airily. "If anything, I am early."

Smiling at his nonsense seemed to be the only possible response. "Is there any point in continuing to argue with you?"

"Probably not," he said with a charming smile. "So, what is my lesson today, O Teacher?"

Flustering sears of heat radiated through her body as Theodosia swallowed.

If she were wise, she would walk away—not just from Albemarle right now, but completely. She should go and find his mother and tell her she had been right. Her son was too much of a challenge, albeit for a different reason.

She could return the money and never again be plagued with desires she must ignore.

If only it were that simple.

"I am ready to pay attention today," he said, a cheeky grin across his face. "Probably."

Not for a long time had Theodosia permitted anyone to get under her skin, but he did. She wanted to be closer to him, and that was a mistake. "Today, we will be practicing the unchaperoned walk."

Albemarle raised an eyebrow. "Goodness, that's a little racy, don't you think?"

It was all she could do not to reach out and take his hand in hers. *Racy?* He had no comprehension of what she wanted.

"The unchaperoned walk is a core part of your courting and is often the best way for two individuals to spend time together without prying eyes," she said sternly. "When we find you a match, you will find this an instrumental tool. You will be expected then, as now, to be a *gentleman*."

He sighed at the emphasis on her last word. "What a shame. I do not think I have ever been a gentleman."

Theodosia smiled. *She could see that quite plainly.* "All the more reason to practice. As I am sure, you are aware in good society, the unchaperoned walk cannot occur at the beginning of an acquaintance with a young lady. That would be most rebellious and radical. It is typically utilized as a prelude to a proposal."

Albemarle's smile did not disappear as he looked around them theatrically. "My word—*we* are not chaperoned! That is most indecorous of you, Miss Ashbrooke."

How did he make her feel so alive with just a few teasing words?

"This is different," she said hastily. "This—this is training. I am your matchmaker, and besides, I have a reputation as such. No one will be surprised or shocked to see us together."

She rose, and Albemarle mirrored her, offering her his arm.

When she hesitated, he said in a low voice, "Go on. I dare you."

Theodosia glared. If they had been alone in his rooms, she would have snapped, given him a tongue lashing to make sure he did not repeat the indignity.

As it was...

Her whole body seemed to shiver as she took his arm, and as they started to walk, she felt the tension leave her frame.

"For a moment there, I thought you were not going to take my arm," he said quietly as they walked through the gardens.

"For a moment there, I thought I wasn't," she admitted. *Why had she revealed that?*

Albemarle's face was a mixture of concern and interest. "You do not trust me."

They reached one end of the gardens and circled about, retracing their steps.

"'Tis not a question of trust."

Silence hung between them for almost a full moment before he tightened his grip on her arm. "Then it is a question of desire?"

Theodosia took a deep breath and glanced at him before responding—and at that moment, she saw the desire in his eyes.

He wanted her. There was no teasing here, no embarrassment at his question, just an earnest request to understand her.

Why was she holding back? Why would she consider opening up to him? Such conflicting emotions warred in her heart, but Theodosia could no longer ignore the feelings he stirred in her.

She swallowed and turned to face the path as she murmured, "Nonsense."

Three pairs of couples walked by, each in earnest conversation.

"This is a time for courting," Albemarle said in a normal voice, as though the last few minutes had not occurred.

"Yes," she said, grasping at a seemingly neutral topic of conversation. "Yes, Sydney Gardens are frequented by many courting couples. Its many open wide spaces make it suitable for—"

"Let's practice courting now," he said, interrupting her in that endearingly irritating way. Lowering his voice, he continued, "Miss Ashbrooke. I am relieved we are alone, finally. I have much to tell you."

This was too intense once again. "Really?"

Albemarle nodded. "About how I feel. About how you make me feel."

The only connection between them was her arm in his, and yet it seemed to overwhelm her. The pressure of his fingers on hers. The little part of her skin that was touching his, a promise of something to come.

If only this were real. If only the words he said meant something. She would give anything—almost anything—for Albemarle to say those words truthfully.

But he was just teasing. *This was just practice, wasn't it?*

She was his matchmaker, and she had to remember that.

"Very good," she said lightly. "But you may wish to slow down there. Your intended bride may not be ready for such protestations of affection."

They had turned a corner into a wooded area. The other people enjoying Sydney Gardens had stayed near the gates. They were alone.

Albemarle stopped. "Theodosia, I am not teasing you."

This could not be permitted to continue. She had to stop it before—

"I cannot believe I am saying this, but...damnit, Theodosia, I have been honest from the start," said Albemarle with a smile. "Theodosia, I want you, not one of the ladies in your damned book!"

"You—you cannot be serious," she stammered, her pounding heart threatening to crack one of her ribs. "You said yourself, you have no wish to get married at all!"

"Can't a man change his mind?" He looked wild. "Marry me, Theodosia."

She pulled her arm away and stepped back. *He was mad. He was jesting! She should laugh—it was a joke.*

Her brittle laughter stopped the moment she saw his expression. Albemarle was rarely serious, but he was now, and there was that desire in his eyes still.

"But I-I...I am a matchmaker, not a countess!" was all she could think to say.

Albemarle smiled. "I could change that."

Theodosia opened her mouth but said nothing. *This was a dream—one of her wild dreams she would never tell anyone.*

She barely knew him. He was teasing her, distracting her from what his mother had paid her to do. She was here to help him find a wife, and she would never marry a client.

The hope that had started to spring inside her was quelled. "Thank you, but no."

Albemarle sighed theatrically. "Damnit, Theodosia, I am serious. More than serious. When are you going to realize I am determined to have you?"

It was almost word for word what Frederick—what *he* had once said to her.

"I have never been more serious, Theodosia. When will you realize I am

determined to have you, no matter what she says?"

She swallowed. She would never allow herself to be vulnerable like that again. She would never let her heart hurt again.

She was a matchmaker—she found matches for others. That was the closest she would get to a proposal.

It was fortuitous that, at that moment, Miss Howarth came into view.

"Miss Howarth!" Theodosia said loudly, almost sagging with relief.

The lady smiled and came closer, evidently intrigued.

"Miss Howarth, the Earl of Lenskeyn," said Theodosia in a hurried rush. "Why do you not walk together for a bit? I have an errand, such a shame I did not recall sooner."

She only risked a brief glance at Albemarle, who looked disappointed.

"Are you sure you will not stay, Miss Ashbrooke?" he asked stiffly. "As a chaperone? I am not sure if I am ready for an unchaperoned walk?"

His words were designed to make her smile, and he was successful, but it was not enough to dissuade her. The best thing she could do was to remove herself from this situation.

As soon as possible.

"Nonsense," she said brusquely. "You have just proven to me you are, and I am sure Miss Howarth has nothing to worry about. Good day, my lord, Miss Howarth."

It took every bit of her will not to look back as she walked away.

CHAPTER EIGHT

"**A**ND THE DRESS! Oh, my lord, the wedding gown is simply sublime. Designed to mirror the wedding cake in every conceivable way, it has tiers of..."

If Miss Lymington did not alter her topic of conversation soon, he was going to achieve what he had considered the impossible and fall asleep standing up.

"Very elegant, I must say," she simpered, looking through delicate lashes. "Naturally, the gown was designed with the church in mind. Have you ever been to St. Anne's? A delightful little place, you can easily miss it if you do not know..."

He swallowed, hoping his glazed expression did not reveal to the young lady just how bored he really was. Footmen passed with platters of sweetmeats and pastries as the music echoed from the room next door.

The dancing had begun, then. Though he would have little chance to dance himself unless he could extricate himself from this outpour of nonsense from Miss Lymington.

"My sister always liked the finer things in life, and with a marriage agreed with the Duke of Larnwick, she can adequately plan for them," she was saying, a little sneer not quite controlled. "That is why the diamonds of his mother have been called from the family vault, of course. She was determined to have them, and I said to her, Issy, diamonds are not the thing you should be mostly concentrating on! But then, how often does one wed a duke?"

Albemarle waited for her to continue and then realized he was expected to contribute at this point. "Oh, yes, to be sure. I cannot think when I ever have wedded a duke."

His sarcasm went utterly unnoticed.

"Well, precisely! But if we are going with diamonds for you, I said, then really pearls on the wedding cake no longer suit. We decided to…"

Albemarle had no idea how to make her stop. He could not recall being so bored in his life—weren't balls in Bath supposed to be wild, adventurous, exciting things?

Countless letters from friends and acquaintances had made their way across the Continent to him in Greece, imploring him to return, teasing him with hints of exuberance, tantalizing details of wild parties.

He raised an eyebrow as he took in the polite clusters of quiet conversation, the lack of good wine, and the sound of cheerful but hardly exuberant dancing in the other room.

Here he was, stuck hearing about a wedding he had no interest in between two people he had never met!

"—and the flowers! I thought lilies would be a little too…well, funereal for a wedding," Miss Lymington continued, dropping her voice a little, "but then, when we visited the wedding florist and saw an example, my lord, it quite took my breath away."

"Indeed."

"Indeed, they did," beamed Miss Lymington, tapping him gently with her fan. "I could not credit it, but there you are, I am wrong sometimes! When our mother heard that…"

Had ladies always been this dull? Albemarle tried to think back to the few ladies he knew and found he could barely recall their conversation. It must be a coincidence, surely, but since his ridiculous marital training had begun with Theodosia—Miss Ashbrooke, he really must remember to call her that in public—every other lady he conversed with simply…

Faded into the background. Their topics of conversation, their choice of language, and most importantly, their ability to keep Albemarle entertained, had all disappeared.

He smiled. *Theo.* She really was one of a kind, and the damned woman should have been here by now. She had said nine o'clock, and it was almost ten now. Why was she always making him wait?

Miss Lymington was smiling. Why was she smiling? *Had she said something witty—should he have laughed?*

Albemarle stiffened as she tapped him with her fan once again. *Christ alive, he had been smiling at the thought of Theo, and now the silly girl thought he was smiling at her!*

"Well, you know what they say," she said with a delicate smile. "Going to one wedding brings on another. My family is so well-practiced in the art of wedding planning now, I hope we will soon be able to put our skills to the test."

What was she driveling about? "Oh, yes?"

She simpered, and Albemarle worked hard not to roll his eyes. *Well, there goes another society miss with completely the wrong idea about his intentions.* Poor Miss Howarth from that irritating card party probably had the same idea—the same incorrect idea, especially after that walk in Sydney Gardens.

He was not about to propose to anyone, and he was damned if he was going to let Theo arrange a bride for him.

Not when his dreams were full of the matchmaker herself...

"When I heard the plans for their honeymoon, I thought—"

"Very crowded, isn't it?" Albemarle interrupted. *It was time to take control of this boring conversation.*

Miss Lymington blinked, evidently thrown by the change in topic. "Crowded?"

He nodded as he grabbed at a glass of wine carried by a passing footman. "Yes, crowded. Many people here at the ball who you know?"

"Not especially, no," Miss Lymington said warily. "I mean, 'tis hardly Almack's. One cannot expect the best people to attend a ball like this, even a private one."

Albemarle hid his smile in his glass. He was not sure whether Braedon, who had put a good deal of work into ensuring his ball was one of the best in the Season, would take too kindly to Miss Lymington's words.

"I am so new to society, I hardly know one face from the other," he said, treating Miss Lymington to a rare smile, which made her simper. "Is there anyone from Lady Romeril's card party here, for instance? We had such a lovely time, did we not?"

Another simper from Miss Lymington and she shifted to be closer to him.

Really, it was all too predictable, thought Albemarle dryly. Poor Miss Lymington. With all her thirty thousand pounds, one would think she would try for a duke, like her twin sister, but she seemed perfectly happy to attempt for him.

It was tiresome. *She* was tiresome, bless her. Any other year, he would have been intrigued by her beauty and wealth enough to entertain the thought of a dalliance, but now...

"—obviously will be here, as 'tis his ball!" Miss Lymington laughed coquettishly. "And Miss Darby is somewhere around here. I am sure I saw her earlier."

"And Miss Ashbrooke?" He had spoken as lightly as possible.

Miss Lymington snorted. "Well, I suppose she could be here, but I never take much notice of servants. Who knows what they get up to?"

The boredom and mild entertainment Albemarle had felt conversing with Miss Lymington evaporated, leaving only a spike of irritation.

Theodosia, a servant? It was wildly inaccurate—worse, it was offensive. Theodosia was a goddess in her own right. He had never known an obsession like this before, and his thoughts were inextricably drawn to her over and over again.

Each time he thought he had stopped thinking about her, he realized he was then congratulating himself, silently, for not remembering the softness of her hands, the arch of her eyebrows, *that cutting way she looked at him that made him feel…*

He swallowed. If he was not careful, he was going to find himself hard, right here at Braedon's damn ball, talking to Miss Lymington! That would certainly convince her of his interest.

As Miss Lymington continued to pout, talking of her gown intended for her sister's nuptials, the memory of that wild proposal in the gardens sparked in his mind.

What had possessed him to propose, for God's sake! Just two weeks ago, he had been protesting to his mother, quite ardently, that he had no desire to marry at all.

Now he had proposed marriage, in complete seriousness—*and the bedeviled woman dared to reject him.*

It was nonsense. It was a sharp kick to his ego and no mistake. And all it did was set his body alight for Miss Theodosia Ashbrooke all the more.

"I am sure I can procure an invitation for you."

"What?" Albemarle blinked. *Invitation? What in God's name for?*

"Why, for my sister's wedding, your lordship," Miss Lymington said with a smile. "I do not know if you are acquainted with His Grace—a rather rough and uncouth fellow if you ask me, but my sister…"

Albemarle tried to pay attention; he really did. But the room was warm, his drink was intoxicating, and Miss Lymington was not. *Why did she drivel on and on about her sister's wedding?*

He had already found his perfect match. If only Theodosia could see it. If only she could see how obvious it was, how they were made for each other. *Her sharp prickles rounding off his edges perfectly.*

"I thought Miss Ashbrooke would be here by now," he said, interrupting a tirade from Miss Lymington about the guest list.

For the first time in their conversation, she frowned. "Miss Ashbrooke, again? If you are so interested in her, why are you talking to me? Ah, I can see Lady Romeril. Do excuse me."

Taking only a moment to curtsey, Miss Lymington strode away in what Albemarle could only describe as a huff. She curtseyed to the older woman and started talking in a hurried, low voice. The two ladies, one young, one approaching seventy, turned to look at him. Both scowled.

Albemarle bowed low with much twirling of his hands and a broad smile, and guffawed as they turned away.

Well, he was unlikely to receive a good report from either of them, and Lady Romeril was one of the key voucher holders for Almack's. He could wave admission to that hallowed ground goodbye.

Like he cared. He had never gone out of his way to earn the good opinion of others. One did not have to when one was an earl, and an errant earl who spent most of his time abroad cared even less.

It had ceased to be meaningful the moment he had said those words to Theodosia in the garden.

"Marry me, Theodosia."

"B-But I-I...I am a matchmaker, not a countess!"

Albemarle placed the now empty wine glass onto a table and sighed heavily. No, he was not here to impress everyone. He was not here to impress anyone.

It was Theodosia he knew he had to convince, and she—

She had just walked into the room, and his heart swelled, pouring affection through his veins and making his legs feel weak.

She was beautiful. Not dressed to impress, she would leave that to the ladies in that damned notebook of hers. No, Theodosia dressed with elegance, restraint, and good taste.

Far more alluring.

Albemarle tried to take a step toward her and realized his cursed legs would not work.

How did a mere matchmaker have this perturbing effect on him? But then, Theodosia was no mere matchmaker. *Mere matchmaker?* She was something entirely different from any woman he had ever encountered.

The Earl of Lenskeyn had been a slave to no one his entire life—but God's teeth, he would be a slave for her.

Albemarle swallowed as he watched her greet the people around her. Everyone was very polite, to be sure, but they seemed to forget about her almost immediately. She was—what had Miss Lymington called her? A servant?

Bile rot. In mere weeks, he had found himself besotted with her.

Albemarle attempted to attract her attention in the only way he knew how.

"Theodosia!"

He cringed at his mistake. The room went silent, heads turning to stare at both of them.

Really, calling a lady by her Christian name in public, shouting it to boot!

A delicate blush blossomed on her cheeks as the matchmaker strode across the room and stopped before him with an almighty glare.

"Now really, you are too much, you foolish man," she said, eyes narrowed. "I did not consider proper deportment and accurate social customs for names to be lessons an earl would require! Perhaps I was mistaken!"

She continued to glare as she waited for his response, but Albemarle had to swallow down his delight before he spoke. *Christ in his Heaven, but no one was like Theodosia when riled up.*

He wanted her. He wanted her writhing underneath him and calling his name. He wanted to taste her, to kiss every inch of her.

But more than that, he wanted this fiery woman by his side for the rest of the years God would permit him.

"You are smiling and not attending," Theodosia said sternly, keeping her voice low to ensure no one else could hear. "I am surprised at you, your lordship. Have I taught you nothing?"

Albemarle swallowed again. *Why did his body react this way, seeing Theodosia furious with him?* There was something delightfully perverse about it. No one told an earl what to do—no one ever had. No one had the guts.

No one except her.

A few curious glances were thrown their way as the matchmaker gave her most prodigious client a good telling off. But there were far more intrigues at a ball than an earl being chastised by a matchmaker.

"See, the entire world is watching."

Albemarle shivered. Theodosia had stepped closer and now whispered in his ear. The softness of her breath on his neck made him almost melt into his boots.

"The news that an earl is looking for a bride has clearly spread," Theodosia said delicately, a little laugh in her voice. "Half a matchmaker's work is done through gossip and tittle-tattle, your lordship, but the rest has to be done by you. Now. Who will you dance with first this evening?"

He knew very much who he would like to dance with. "Who's to say I have not already danced with someone?"

Theodosia moved away, maintaining the proper etiquette of a ball. "I do. I know you, Albemarle Howard, and I would bet—not my entire savings, but a significant portion, that you have stood here making banal conversation with whoever walked up to you. Am I right?"

He could not help himself. The words spilled out of his mouth before he could catch them. "Dance with me."

The smile on Theodosia's face disappeared immediately, but he could see the desire in her eyes.

"Damn your self-control, that restraint forbidding you from enjoying anything in life," he said in a low voice, his hand finding hers. "I asked you because I want to dance with you. No tricks, no hidden agenda."

Theodosia was unsure. It did not take a ladies' man to see she had been hurt. At some point in her past, a brigand had hurt her, and if he ever met that sorry fool, he would—

But this was not the time to throw around threats. This was his chance to show Theodosia some men could be trusted.

He wanted her. He would have her. It was as simple as that.

"Fine," she said eventually, "but only as a practice. I have not seen you dance before, and you need further instruction."

"No, as a woman I am courting," Albemarle said firmly, his fingers interlocking with hers close to his side so that no one could see. "Miss Ashbrooke...Theodosia."

He could not continue. Her name on his lips overwhelmed him. He needed to regain control of himself. *He was a Lenskeyn!*

"I am not sure how else to show you I am serious about this suit," he murmured, his eyes never leaving her. "I meant what I said in Sydney Gardens. I want to dance with you, court you, wed you, damn it all. Why are you so obstinate? Isn't this your bloody job, finding me a bride?"

The curse words fell from his mouth with frustration, but Theodosia did not pull away. "I suppose so, but that bride is not supposed to be me."

"Where is it written?" he challenged. *He would convince her, if it were the last thing he did at this dull ball.* "I am determined. You are a far better match for me than any chit of a thing you could find, and I am not about to accept defeat. So."

Dropping her hand, he held out his arm. She paused for what felt an inordinate amount of time and then took it.

Every inch of Albemarle's body came alive. Before he knew it, they were standing in the line of dancers, and Theodosia was stepping forward, hands outstretched, to take his own.

Each time they touched, burning pain in his chest radiated across his entire body. The first time it occurred, Albemarle was convinced it was a heart attack. He was aging, yes, but he had not considered himself old.

But then his gaze connected with hers, laughing as she twisted around, weaving in and out of the others in the dance, and a jolt fired in his stomach.

Hell's bells. Albemarle knew what that meant. He knew love when it twisted his stomach in knots and made him furious at any and every other gentleman for touching her.

Theodosia Ashbrooke. She had found a way into his heart, cheeky, forceful, direct woman that she was. She used none of her feminine wiles, utterly avoided bringing any notice to herself, but as Albemarle turned and brought her into his arms as they paraded down the set, he knew this was where she belonged.

In his arms.

Life would never be the same again—and life would hardly be worth living if it did not have Theodosia in it.

Before he could understand the thoughts and feelings rushing through his mind, before he could enjoy the dance or say something witty—or say anything, any words at all!—it was over. They were bowing and curtseying along with the rest of the set, applauding the musicians for their tune.

Albemarle watched her, laughing, cheeks flushed, speaking with the lady beside her. She was radiant. She was everything he wanted, everything he had not known he had wanted.

Christ alive, he was in trouble now.

"Well, as practice, that was...good." Theodosia smiled and then laughed as she stepped toward him. "I believe the dance has entirely exhausted you! Go and find some refreshment, your lordship—I was rather late to the ball, so I need to circulate. Ask a lady to dance."

She had stepped away before Albemarle could find the words to tell her how he felt. He barely understood it himself, except that he would have her.

For the next two excruciating hours, he was forced to watch Theodosia go to work. She was an expert, almost an extension of the dance as she wove in and out of people, speaking to some, encouraging others.

Albemarle could not tear his eyes from her. She made introductions, met new people, and ensured she gained the most critical details from them, found some who were a little lost in the crowd, and made sure they were moved to a lively group.

She was a master—no, a mistress of society. He was drawn to her like a moth to flame. Everywhere she went were the best conversations, the funniest jokes, the most interesting discussions.

She knew everyone or could be introduced to anyone and was the matchmaker for society, evidently, for a reason.

Albemarle marveled and felt jealous of everyone she was with in equal measures. No matter who attempted to draw him into conversation, it was utterly useless. He could hardly string six words together, his attention captured by the woman who protested she had no interest in him.

If he had hoped for a woman who was his equal in intellect, passion, determination, and fire, then he had found her. If only he were clever enough to persuade Theodosia that she was, in truth, his perfect match.

When he saw her mutter something low to a footman and, in turn, receive her pelisse, Albemarle was forced from his stupor.

"You are going?" he said after stepping across the room to her side.

Theodosia smiled wearily. "I am tired, your lordship. My first appointment this morning was before nine o'clock, and it is past midnight now. It all starts again tomorrow, so I must be leaving. Did you make any interesting connections? Speak to any ladies who took your fancy?"

Ignoring the questions entirely, Albemarle said, "You cannot be walking back to your rooms? Here, my carriage is waiting outside, and my horses receive very little exercise. Let them take you home."

They had stepped outside now, and the chilling midnight air brought a blush to her cheeks. He saw her hesitate. A carriage would be much more comfortable than a walk.

"There is nothing untoward about my offer," he said in a low voice, attempting to win her around, "especially as you are in my employ."

Christ and all his disciples, why did he say that? Thrown into agonies of shame, he saw Theodosia's cheeks pink a little more, but then she nodded.

"'Tis a cold night," she said formally, "and I would be grateful of your carriage, your lordship."

Albemarle nodded, barely trusting himself not to say something foolish. Raising his hand in the air, James immediately clicked at the horses, bringing the Lenskeyn carriage around to them. Opening the door, he offered his hand, but she had already clambered in.

He smiled. *Of course, Miss Theodosia Ashbrooke does not need assistance.*

"Miss Theodosia Ashbrooke," he murmured to his driver. "Queen's Square. Take the longest route possible."

Following her into the carriage, he tapped the roof, and it shuddered into motion.

"The longest route possible?" Theodosia smiled. She was seated beside him. "My, my, with anyone else, I would be concerned, your lordship."

"Perhaps you should be."

She laughed, pulling off her gloves and placing them in her reticule. "Now then, your lordship, we are alone. You do not have to practice your little patter on me."

This was it; his chance to show her, not attempt to tell her what was stirring within him.

"Theodosia," he whispered.

She looked at him, her eyes intrigued and suddenly uncertain.

"There..." Albemarle swallowed. *No creative words, just the truth.* "There is nothing in the world I want more than you, right now."

Any lady would be shocked to hear such words, but Theodosia smiled. "I know."

There was desire in her eyes—Albemarle could not mistake it. She wanted him, and his heart soared as he acted on instinct and instinct alone.

He moved closer, shifting slowly as though she was a fox in the wild, and he was hunting her. She did not move away.

And then she was in his arms, his lips on hers, and it was so heavenly, he almost cried out with the perfection of it. Theodosia was just as eager for him, pulling him closer with her arms around his neck. Albemarle could not think; he could only feel, and what a feeling!

Her lips parted, welcoming him in, and she moaned a little as he teased her tongue with his own, worshipping her. His hands were around her waist, pulling her closer, so she was in his lap in a moment, utterly his, only his, and would be his for the rest of their—

The carriage came to a juddering halt, and they broke apart.

"What the devil is going on?" Albemarle muttered wildly, looking out of the window. "Why have we stopped?"

"We have arrived," said Theodosia breathlessly.

"Arrived? At your rooms?"

She nodded, shifting so she rubbed against his manhood, and he groaned and buried his face in her neck.

He wanted to go in with her. He wanted her to ask him in, for them to continue their kissing and for it to lead somewhere more. *Somewhere with far fewer clothes on.*

"Don't go."

The words were breathed rather than said and came from somewhere vulnerable inside him. He did not want to part with her. He could not countenance losing her, not yet.

There was something unfathomable in her gaze. Something fierce and wild but untamable.

She did not speak but slowly lowered her lips onto his and took possession of them, utterly controlling the kiss that grew deeper and deeper as her hand teased the nape of his neck.

And for goodness knows how long, for Albemarle could have sworn time had stopped in that carriage, they lost themselves in kisses that said far more than words ever could.

CHAPTER NINE

THE INSTANT THEODOSIA sipped her tea, she regretted it. The scalding liquid burned her tongue, robbing it of all sensation but pain. Managing to keep quiet in the almost silent drawing room of Lady Howard, she placed the cup back in its saucer and waited for her tea to cool down.

Her tongue still burned, but it was still not as hot as when Albemarle had kissed her in that carriage.

"There is nothing in the world I want more than you, right now."

Her cheeks warmed. Theodosia glanced around the drawing room quickly, but none of the ladies present seemed to have noticed anything was amiss with the demure matchmaker.

This was a very different type of affair than many of her social occasions. At nine and twenty, Theodosia was at a rather discomforting age. One of the oldest when with the young ladies of the town, far too young to be one of the matrons.

Add in her seniority in society as a matchmaker, but her inferiority as an unmarried and childless woman…

She sighed. She should be grateful to be invited anywhere at all. This particular gathering was a stroke of luck. Lady Howard had mentioned it in passing at Viscount Braedon's ball, and Theodosia had cleverly won herself an invitation.

All the fashionable Mamas were here—Mrs. Lymington, Mrs. Chesworth, Mrs. Howarth. Perfect for Theodosia, still struggling for eligible young ladies.

"And what marvelous weather we are having, for the time of year," Mrs. Chesworth was saying loudly enough to ensure she controlled all the conversation in the room. "Keeping the gentlemen in the country, of course, which is a real shame. My son-in-law—the Duke of Axwick, you must know him—has delayed his plans to arrive in town twice."

Theodosia hid a smile as she listened. How like Mrs. Chesworth to casually mention her daughter's husband like that, but then, what society mother did not delight in showing off to friends and enemies alike? And with a son-in-law who was a duke, there was no end of opportunities for Mrs. Chesworth to ensure her acquaintance knew just how fortunate she was.

"I thought her behavior very vulgar," said Lady Romeril on the other side of the room, holding court with a deferential Mrs. Marnion. "And when I say vulgar, I mean it. I mean, dressed up to the nines at another lady's engagement picnic! If he had not married Miss Seton, it would have been a scandal…"

Yes, it was true. Miss Priscilla Seton had acted far more wildly than society ever could accept, but she had married her man. In the eyes of the *ton*, that meant almost everything was forgivable.

But not, it appeared, in the eyes of Lady Romeril.

"I would not have countenanced such behavior if it had been my house," she was saying to the rapt Mrs. Marnion. "But then, Lady Audley, my cousin, you know, always had a very *particular* way of doing things."

She sighed impressively, leaving Mrs. Marnion and any other Lady Howard guests who were listening in no doubt of her opinion.

Theodosia smiled. Her settee was comfortable, and she had been on her feet all day, up and down Bath, conducting interviews for potential new clients. It was rather peaceful, seated here amid mature womanhood, with nothing to distract her.

Almost nothing. Unbidden, the memories of kissing Albemarle quite disgracefully in his carriage resurfaced once again.

She shivered. The memory of his hands around her body, his lips kissing a trail down her neck…

She should not have kissed him. It was most indecorous, and worse, he would now have quite the wrong idea about her intentions. She had meant what she said to him that day in the garden after his ridiculous proposal, that she could not possibly even consider it.

Theodosia was his matchmaker. Earls did not marry matchmakers!

That had been three days ago. Se had managed to keep her hands away from him during that time—although she had been forced to avoid his a few times, hating herself, knowing all she wanted was to give in to temptation.

But she must not. As Theodosia drank her tea, thankfully now cool enough to swallow, she tried not to think of the Earl of Lenskeyn.

It was easier said than done. Her host, Lady Howard, was Albemarle's sister-in-law, widow to his brother. There was a painting of the two brothers on the wall, painted at least twenty years ago, but one could still see the handsome man she knew so well in the youthful face of the elder boy.

"And I hear your eldest is to be married!"

"No, actually, 'tis my second—but they are twins, you see, so in many ways, it hardly matters which is to marry first," corrected Mrs. Lymington with a self-satisfied smile. "The Duke of Larnwick, don't you know? A fine man, such a good connection for our Isabella. Still, we must find a good match for Olivia! Our youngest is not out, and…"

Theodosia made a mental note to inquire, delicately, of course, as to the youngest Miss Lymington's age. If Miss Isabella Lymington were to be married soon, then there would be another Lymington available to join Theodosia's circle.

Too rich for poor Mr. Birch's youngest, and too plain, if the rumors were true, for Mr. Croft. If she had the same dowry as her older sisters, perhaps one for…

Theodosia swallowed. Well. *Albemarle.* There would be at least twenty years between them, but that had not stopped many a societal match. Indeed, some marriages were all the better for the husband having a few more years of maturity and wisdom.

The thought of introducing the earl to the youngest Miss Lymington made her stomach churn.

Was it not enough that she was so indecorous as to kiss one of her clients? A gentleman for whom she should be spending every waking hour finding a bride for? No, it was worse. She was even considering *not* introducing him to ladies who would be most suitable, just because she felt…

Attached to him. She would not permit herself to consider it any more than that.

"And there is no animosity between your girls?" Mrs. Coulson asked skeptically. "No ill-feeling between Isabella and Olivia, for example, due to the younger getting married before the elder?"

There was too much of hesitation from Mrs. Lymington for her next words to be credible. "No, to be sure, no animosity whatsoever. They are the best of friends, always have been, and I am sure always will."

Theodosia smiled as she sipped her tea. One of the wonderful things about gatherings like this, and she had to applaud Lady Howard for its organization, was to invite just enough people who liked the sound of their own voices. Lady Romeril and Mrs. Chesworth were perfect examples of this. They could continue conversations in empty rooms, and the gentle chatter ensured that ladies like herself could merely sit and enjoy the afternoon.

Mrs. Marnion moved to help herself to more tea on the sideboard, and the portrait of the Howard brothers came into Theodosia's focus again.

She smiled as she looked into the painted gaze of Albemarle.

She prided herself on her ability to judge a gentleman, often within minutes. From the end of her first interview with Albemarle and his mother, she had known he was rude, arrogant, opinionated, and dismissive of others.

The more she became acquainted with him, the more she saw through that façade. True, he was rude and considered his opinions far superior to those around him.

But those were merely shields designed to keep out the world. The earl had hidden from society, and so society had deemed him as unworthy of its attention.

Whether it was her directness, her forcefulness, her inability to be cowed by him...Theodosia did not know. However she had done it, she had broken through the barrier Albemarle had put up against the world and seen him for who he was.

And liked him. Was attracted to him, in fact, a thought that made her whole body shiver.

He made her smile. He said the things she only thought. In a life ruled by convention and society's expectations, Theodosia had rarely done anything she wanted just for herself.

Albemarle did. He made her want to throw off her shawl and go dancing in the rain.

When would she see him again? They were both invited to another party in a few days, she had seen to that—but she ached for him now. Not just his kisses, which she had decidedly promised herself she would not permit herself to enjoy again, but for his company. His laugh. His sarcastic view of the world that did not darken it but merely illuminated it in a new way.

"Marry me, Theodosia."

She smiled. After kissing for nigh on twenty minutes in his carriage right outside her rooms, perhaps she should start to take his protestations of affection seriously. After all, she could not continue to just kiss the man in secret.

At some point, she would have to make a decision. Maybe—

"Miss Ashbrooke? Are you quite well?"

Theodosia blinked. Their host was in mourning, a gown of the deepest black flowing down her, making her young face look far more lined. She was staring at Theodosia with a concerned expression, and all the other ladies in the room were staring, too.

The rare sensation of discomfort in a public setting crept over her, prickling her skin and making her corset feel a little too tight.

But she was not society's most prodigious matchmaker for nothing.

"I do apologize," she said gracefully, smiling around at the ladies. "I must admit myself utterly absorbed in thoughts of the Seton wedding and how wonderful it was. One of the risks of being such a successful matchmaker, I suppose!"

A few of the ladies smiled, while Lady Romeril snorted and muttered something to Mrs. Marnion.

Mrs. Chesworth did not look convinced and said tartly, "Ah, but it was not the wedding you had originally organized, was it? That poor Miss Lloyd, I wonder what she thought of it all!"

It was not a new perspective to Theodosia, for she had heard it before, whispered when others thought she could not hear them.

And of course, Mrs. Chesworth's only daughter was already married, removing the need for a matchmaker to befriend her. That meant she could be direct with the woman—although careful, naturally, to ensure that any other mamas in the room did not hear her.

After all, her son-in-law was the Duke of Axwick, and little Tabby Chesworth had managed that on her own. Theodosia could not help but be impressed, nor wonder whether the duke could introduce a few more ladies into her circle.

"No, it was not the originally planned wedding—to the untrained eye," Theodosia said smoothly, reaching for her cup of tea. "But what I needed to do was make Charles—I beg your pardon, the Duke of

Orrinshire—come to his senses. He needed to discover on his own, with a little help of course, that the woman he really wanted and was best suited to was right before him."

"Indeed," said Mrs. Chesworth haughtily.

Yes, the Orrinshire affair had been far wilder than most of her matches typically were, but there was always an anomaly now and again.

Theodosia took a sip of tea before nodding. "It was a close call in the end, far closer than I had expected, but the right people wed in the end."

She was gratified to see a few nodding heads of agreement around the room and had to hide her smile as Mrs. Chesworth rose, looking a little ruffled, to help herself to more tea from the corner of the room.

As the conversation in the room grew, Theodosia helped herself to another biscuit. The sugary confection crumbled in her mouth, and she closed her eyes, losing herself in the taste.

Money was never exactly restricted. After paying off those foolish acquired debts, she made a good living from her work and had been careful in saving a fair amount each time a bill was paid. She had a tidy little nest egg that should see her through retirement if she ever decided to retire.

That approach did mean, however, that biscuits, cakes, and other sweet things were few and far between at home. Any opportunity to taste their delights...

"I must say, I did not realize you took such a close interest in the relationships of your clients," said Mrs. Lymington, rising from her seat to position herself closer to the matchmaker. "You seem...well, so absorbed by them."

Theodosia nodded. *The poor woman.* Four daughters, and even with dowries of thirty thousand pounds each, there were few eligible men of that weight to go around.

"Yes," she said aloud, "I dedicate myself to my clients, much like a mother would. In many ways, they become my children. I have no offspring of my own, you see, and so I take them under my wing and try to find the best places for them to be happy. 'Tis a rewarding thing to do in life."

The conversation seemed to have focused on her for far longer than anyone else, and Theodosia was starting to feel a little strange. It was rare that she was in the limelight.

"Tell me about Miss Isabella's wedding plans," she said to Mrs. Lymington, knowing full well this topic would entertain both of them and, most importantly, remove the spotlight from herself.

But before Mrs. Lymington could open her mouth, another voice spoke out.

"I heard that earl is giving you some trouble."

Both Theodosia and Mrs. Lymington looked around to see Mrs. Marnion with an eyebrow raised.

"That's what many people tell me," she continued, elegantly sipping her tea with her little finger sticking out.

A rush of heat had flowed through Theodosia the moment Albemarle was hinted at. The idea that she was now a topic of gossip herself purely because of his antics...well, she should not be surprised. It was a little scandalous, however, for Mrs. Marnion to bring it up at Lady Howard's tea party. Why, she was his sister-in-law.

Theodosia glanced at Lady Howard, but she did not appear to mind. She was sitting alone, watching the world go by through the window.

"No, of course not," Theodosia said aloud, knowing Mrs. Marnion and probably half the room were waiting for her response. "I will find someone for him, eventually. 'Tis vital, as I am sure you can understand, Mrs. Marnion, that the suitability of his partner is balanced. An earl, you see..."

She allowed her voice to trail off delicately, hoping that would be the end of the conversation.

"Albemarle Howard, Earl of Lenskeyn," said Lady Romeril quietly.

"Yes, I know of whom we are speaking," said Theodosia a little tartly. *Well, really! Did the old baggage think she could not keep up?* "He is a little difficult at times, and admittedly is not to everyone's tastes. Nevertheless, I am sure I will find someone who will put up with him."

She laughed at the jest, but no one else in the room laughed with her.

It was at that moment that Lady Howard turned around and said, "Albemarle."

The hairs on the back of Theodosia's neck prickled. *It could not be—fate would not be so cruel as to...*

Turning, she saw Albemarle standing behind her, that crooked smile on his face, which he always had when looking at her. Her heart fluttered, breath caught in her throat.

He was smiling with that self-satisfied look, and she hurriedly tried to recall what she had just said as her cheeks burned.

"He is a little difficult at times, and admittedly is not to everyone's tastes. Nevertheless, I am sure I will find someone who will put up with him."

Theodosia swallowed. She was falling in love with him. There was no other explanation for this rush of feeling each time she saw him, the utterly unmanageable man that he was.

What was the one rule she had given herself, all those years ago when she had first started out as matchmaker—the rule she had never broken?

Never fall in love with the client.

But Albemarle did not make it easy for her. There was something about him no other gentleman had ever sparked in her. Something very similar to a feeling she thought she would never feel again.

Every inch of her was on fire as she stared, transfixed. *She was falling in love with him.*

His smile broadened. "I do hope, Lady Howard, you do not mind if a gentleman 'not to everyone's tastes' joins the party?"

Theodosia whipped around to look at his sister-in-law, who smiled wanly and rose from her seat by the window.

"Of course not," she said quietly. "No brother-in-law of mine will ever be unwelcome here. Do you know Mrs. Lymington?"

With all the gracefulness of a well-practiced hostess, she swept the earl toward the woman in the room with the richest unmarried daughters. Theodosia had to give her that; the woman was a natural.

"You know, I have not yet had the immense pleasure," said Albemarle smoothly, taking the hand of the woman and kissing it gently. "But I have to admit, I have had the pleasure of speaking with your daughter, Miss Olivia, and what a charming woman she has grown to be."

Mrs. Lymington simpered and invited him to sit beside her, proudly looking around the room to ensure everyone heard the compliment the earl had given her daughter.

"Now, you must tell me," he continued, leaning slightly toward her and placing his hand on her arm, "how you managed to have so many pretty daughters and keep so much of your own beauty! You are a marvel, Mrs. Lymington. Do tell us how you did it."

Theodosia watched in horror as Albemarle started to charm Mrs. Lymington. He used all the tricks she had taught him, flattery, careful listening, compliments, the gentle hand on the arm—everything!

She should have been proud. She should have been silently applauding Albemarle for his excellent command of the skills he had learned in only a few weeks.

But shards of jealousy were stabbing through her heart. *How could he speak to her like that, be that close to her when she was just a few feet away!*

Worse, why did she feel so intensely jealous of a woman who was twenty years older than her and already married, to boot!

It was foolish. It was childishness of the worst kind, and Theodosia knew better than that.

At least her mind did. Her heart had a life entirely of its own, and it was furious at him for treating her no better than a simple voyeur of his conversation with Mrs. Lymington.

After the woman had accepted the pretty compliments of the earl, he said, "You must excuse me, Mrs. Lymington—I wish to hear so much more, but I am parched and must help myself to a cup of tea."

He rose, bowed—causing a giggle from the matronly woman—and strode across the room to where the tea things had been left.

In an instant, Theodosia had joined him.

"And what do you think you are doing?" she hissed under the noise of pouring tea.

Albemarle grinned as her stomach swooped. "This is what you wanted, Miss Ashbrooke. You wanted me to find a woman, and that is what I am doing."

"But..." she spluttered. "This was not what I meant! Mrs. Lymington?"

He carefully dropped four sugar cubes into his cup and started to stir. "If you had accepted me," he continued in a low voice, "you would not have to watch this. I asked you to marry me, and you said—"

"Nonsense, that wasn't a real proposal!"

"Wasn't it?" He stared with fierce eyes, and Theodosia found herself unable to speak. "You trained me to find a wife. You encouraged me to go out and charm ladies. If you do not like it..."

Theodosia swallowed. *She did not like it.* She hated it—but to admit why would be to give him power she simply could not accept.

She would not be the fool again.

"And despite being 'not to everyone's tastes,' as you so delicately put it, I think a few women find I do have some charming points," he said in a low voice as he piled biscuits on his saucer. "Remember, Miss Ashbrooke, I am busy finding a bride. At your insistence."

Before she could think of what to say, he was gone.

"Now tell me, Mrs. Lymington," he said loudly, ensuring she could hear every word. "You have more than one beautiful unmarried daughter, do you not?"

It was impossible to watch. The irritating man was not only demonstrating he could be charming, but his words were ringing in her ears.

"I asked you to marry me, and you said—"

"Nonsense, that wasn't a real proposal!"

"Wasn't it?"

If he was in earnest…if he had indeed meant that proposal…

Theodosia moved with her cup of tea back to her seat, close enough to hear every word the earl and Mrs. Lymington exchanged.

Had she been rash to think he would not consider her a suitable wife? Had she been foolish to ignore him, consider him jesting when he had said he wanted to marry her?

That kiss. Those kisses in the carriage, they were burned into her memory.

"Yes, I have my very own matchmaker," said Albemarle with a smile, glancing at her. "She works hard on my behalf to find ladies suitable for me to marry, but I think I have done far better than her so far."

Theodosia smiled and inclined her head. Well, she may be a matchmaker, beneath many of those in society as far as they were concerned, but she was educated, charming, and had more connections in the *ton* than anyone.

Two could play at this game.

CHAPTER TEN

"**Y**OU ABSOLUTE RASCAL! You dog, Braedon—I am not sure whether you're allowed to make that sort of joke in polite company!"

Albemarle laughed heartily, feeling the chuckle right in the depths of his bones as the three gentlemen finished a round of cards in Boodle's, their club. Abraham Fitzclarence, Viscount Braedon, had just told the most raucous joke—one that even he had never heard before, and he ten years the man's senior—and their chuckles had raised some eyebrows in the place.

Braedon grinned. "I was not aware I was in polite company!"

Albemarle laughed again, reaching for his glass of wine that was far emptier than it should have been. Shrugging, he threw the final dregs down his throat and reached for the bottle.

It was empty.

"Damn and blast it, is that another one gone?" he said mildly. "Nothing for it but to open another one."

As if by magic, a footman appeared at his side and proffered another bottle of the most excellent vintage that Montague Cavendish, Duke of Devonshire, had chosen at the beginning of their evening.

Albemarle nodded, but Braedon looked a little hesitant.

"Now then, steady on chaps," he said awkwardly. "The 1749, again? I mean, my pockets aren't lined with gold like yours…"

Money was not something Albemarle had ever concerned himself with, and though these two gentlemen had been friends for a while, it was still a topic rarely breached.

"Think of it as a gift, old boy, and one that you have well-earned," said Devonshire with a hearty laugh. "One from me, an old married man, to you two rapscallions who are unwed and unshackled!"

The footman nodded and pulled out the cork and offered it to Devonshire to taste, but the man waved it away.

"I am sure Boodle's would not offer me corked wine," he said airily. "And grab another bottle of it, too. I have the feeling we may need it sooner than we think."

Braedon's anxious face relaxed immediately. "Why, thank you, Devonshire—and fear not, I will attempt to rob you of some coin so I can pay you back!"

The three men laughed as Devonshire started to deal out the next hand. Albemarle leaned back, his shoulders relaxing. *Well, it was certainly a spot of luck finding these two.* He had hoped there would be a few gentlemen he could sit with at his club. He had been a member for years, despite living on the wrong Continent to just pop in for an afternoon nap.

And here were Braedon and Devonshire, two gentlemen of good family, good repute, and sufficient funds to be members of this hallowed ground, even if Devonshire was rolling in more gold than he knew what to do with and Braedon was obviously a little short at times.

They were delightful company, and right now, that was all that mattered. He was tired of ladies, of society primping and preening, of always being watched, measured, and sized up for so-and-so's daughter or the niece of what's-her-name.

Here, in the club, he could retreat from polite society and play a few hands of cards without being concerned about marriage, or Theodosia, or...

He groaned as he picked up his cards.

"Careful, old chap, or you'll be giving away your hand before we've even started!" Braedon chuckled, throwing down a shilling as his opening bet. "And you've had such a good poker face until now!"

Albemarle smiled mechanically and matched with a shilling of his own. *No, it was not the cards that had caused such a heavy sigh.* Despite all his finer feelings, he had still managed to think about Theodosia.

What was that—the fifth time in the hour? A quick glance to the grandfather clock told him it was, and the minute hand only just starting to rise toward the hour.

Theodosia. What a woman, a fiery thing when riled. He could not help but smile as he remembered how he had teased her when making that disgusting cup of tea, pouring in more milk and sugar than could be stomached, just to prolong their conversation.

"Nonsense, that wasn't a real proposal!"

"Wasn't it?"

"Come on now, Lenskeyn, you need to pay attention if you want to win this hand!" The reprimand was kindly spoken by Devonshire, who had evidently raised the bet and was eagerly looking to see if the older man would match him.

Albemarle folded. He could barely concentrate anyway. His mind was utterly transfixed on the memory of Theodosia.

Her frustration had been palpable—*anything to force a reaction from her.* Theodosia was a block of ice most of the time, and he still had no idea how they had ended up kissing in his carriage after Braedon's ball.

Polite company separated them, her own finer feelings kept them apart, but when all the rules and restrictions were removed, Theodosia was just as wild, just as passionate as he had imagined.

He shifted in his seat, his body reacting to the mere memory of that moment. *Theodosia, in his lap in the carriage, kissing him as though her life depended on it.*

It had been agony to see her at his sister-in-law's, all restraint and respectability.

He really should go and thank Lady Howard at some point for

permitting him to stay. Widowed only a month ago, and he had barely gone to see her to make sure she was managing.

Especially if the rumors were true and she was pregnant. An heir to the Lenskeyn line. It would remove all need for him to marry, change the shape of everything in the family. *His mother would be thrilled.*

A jolt went through him. If Lady Howard *was* pregnant, he would no longer need a matchmaker. Theodosia would be released from his services. Could he then court her, as a woman, as she deserved?

"I said, are you ready for another round?"

Albemarle started, finding both gentlemen staring at him. "W-What?"

"You have not been paying attention," said Braedon with a grin, pulling a pile of silver and a few gold coins toward him. "This blaggard was convinced I could have nothing greater than two pair, and so foolishly overbid his hand. Now, how much was that bottle of wine, Devonshire?"

"Oh, think nothing of it," Devonshire shrugged. "I certainly won't."

Was it Albemarle's imagination, or was there a hint of frustration in the viscount's face as the richer man shrugged off the debt as inconsequential?

What a strange world, he mused. When two gentlemen right at the pinnacle of society, admired by many, considered equals save for mere differences in title, can be friends and yet have a sense of discomfort around money.

Money. He had never been concerned about it. The Lenskeyn estates were plentiful and bountiful, and it cost very little to live abroad. He was probably richer now than he would have been if he had stayed in merry old England.

"Well," he said aloud to clear the tension in the air, "if you are both ready to lose a little more money, I am willing to take it from you."

Braedon, flushed with his recent victory, said, "You believe your luck can hold? You were bound to lose on the last round. You folded so quickly!"

Albemarle said nothing but reached forward and revealed his cards. A straight flush.

Devonshire chuckled as Braedon said, "B-But...but you would have beaten me, Lenskeyn! Why in the devil's name did you fold?"

He shrugged. "I was not sure whether my luck would hold."

"Your luck does not seem to be holding with the ladies, at any rate," said Devonshire with a grin. "That's what Harry tells me, and she is never wrong."

Albemarle frowned. "Harry? She?"

"His wife," supplied Braedon as he dealt again. "Lady Harriet Stanhope, as was. 'Harry' to her friends. 'Her Grace' to us plebs."

"Oh shut up, you've known Harry since the Ark," Devonshire said, looking at his cards and rearranging them in his hand. "I heard you had engaged a matchmaker, Lenskeyn, but she too is finding it difficult to find anyone who will put up with you!"

The two gentlemen guffawed, and Albemarle joined them with a smile. He could hardly disagree with them. *Not even Theodosia would agree to marry him, and she was the one who was supposed to be championing him to the women of society!*

"I am just biding my time," he said aloud, knowing the two gentlemen would continue to jest until he responded. "I have already found the woman I want, and so it is just a matter of time before I convince her. Why else do you think I am able to relax this evening with the two of you?"

Braedon laughed as he threw down half a guinea. "God's teeth, that is bad news."

Albemarle frowned as he matched the bet. "Bad news?"

The viscount nodded with a smile. "Well, think about it, Lenskeyn. If a gentleman such as yourself, with titles, connections, wealth, and the maturity and wisdom of years, struggles to convince a girl into marriage—well, what hope have the rest of us got?"

"Now, are we playing cards, or aren't we?" interrupted Devonshire, who had an eager look on his face. *He must have a good hand,* Albemarle thought. "Remember, aces are high, and sevens are wicked, and anyone with the queen of hearts, in honor of our newest friend, takes all."

"The queen of hearts, you say?" said Braedon delicately with a knowing smile.

Albemarle worked hard to keep his face straight. Braedon was a fool, but a young fool, so he was likely to grow out of it. His bluff was pathetic, really—or at least, it was when Albemarle was looking at the queen of hearts in his hand.

"Well, if Braedon has the queen, I suppose we should just fold," he said airily.

"No, let's continue," Braedon said hastily. "I shall not play it unless in a run. Agreed?"

Devonshire looked shrewdly. "You promise not to play the queen?"

Braedon nodded, and Albemarle had to stifle a laugh with a swig of red wine. *Really, it was too easy.* When the pups were at least a decade younger than him, they had much to learn when it came to bluffing. They could bet themselves into a frenzy, and then he would swoop in with the queen and take it all.

"Right, in that case, I bid another half guinea," he said loudly. "Will you chaps match me, or…"

His voice trailed away—it was that or start to shout. There was a commotion occurring in the adjoining room at the club, and so many people were starting to gasp, shout, or yell, that it was quite impossible to hear each other properly.

"What the devil do you think is going on?" Braedon managed to shout across the tumult.

Albemarle shrugged. *Finally, a hand he knew he could not lose, and they were getting distracted by a mere scuffle in another room.* "Match my half guinea?" he roared.

But Devonshire was not paying attention. He had turned in his chair and was peering across the room to see whether he could make out what was going on.

As the noise quieted down a little, he said, "What do you think is going on through there?"

"Probably someone has dropped an expensive bottle of wine," said Braedon with a laugh. "And now the damned fools are arguing over who should pay for it."

Devonshire chuckled, but Albemarle was far more focused on the game than on the noise. As that very thought crossed his mind, he heard a voice emerge over the outcry.

It sounded like...

The door to their room burst open, and a few gentlemen seated closer to it cried out in shock and surprise. It was a woman—a woman at Boodle's! The club had never admitted ladies, and never would.

But this was not just any lady. It was Theodosia Ashbrooke, and a Theodosia that Albemarle hardly recognized.

Gone was the drab gown, carefully chosen to fade into the background. Gone was the delicate but simple hair, the lack of jewelry, and the smart but practical pelisse.

This one was attired as though for a ball at St. James's Court. Her gown was a light, cream silk that shone in the candlelight, small pearls embroidered across the bodice and the sleeves. Pearls hung in flowing strands down her front and were pinned into her hair, which had been curled and dressed in the latest style.

But perhaps most surprising of all was her expression. Whenever Albemarle had seen Theodosia, she had either been glaring at him, smiling at ladies she was introducing to him, or...well, *kissing him.*

She smiled, a mischievous lilt to her lips, looking utterly possessed in a sea of gentlemen calling for her to be removed.

"Hello, my lord," she said softly.

Albemarle laughed. *What had he got into with this wild woman?* Beautiful beyond compare, fastidious to the point of death about the rules of society, and here she was, breaking all of them.

And she knew it. He could see it in the high color of her cheeks and the way she resolutely looked at him and no one else.

For all her talk of society's rules, she knew how to make a scene.

"My God, a woman!" Braedon said, his mouth open, his eyes dancing with mischief. "We can't have that. Where will it end! You're not permitted to be in here, woman!"

This last sentence was directed toward Theodosia, who raised an eyebrow majestically. "Really? How interesting."

Not another single syllable passed her lips as she delicately walked across the room, ignoring the gasps and mutterings from the other gentlemen, and sat herself down in the empty seat at the card table—right beside Albemarle.

"Hallo, Miss Ashbrooke," said Devonshire with a grin. It was clear he had no fear of the matchmaker, nor any interest in the spectacle coming to a quick end. "Careful, if my wife gets wind of this, she'll be here before you can say lickety-split. She always said the rules were archaic."

"I always knew Lady Devonshire had excellent taste," smiled Theodosia, her body resolutely turned toward Albemarle. "But I am afraid I have not come here to make a scene. I am merely here on a matter of business."

"Business?" Albemarle had managed to hold his tongue until this point, but he could not bear to be left out of the conversation any longer. *Damnit, she was his Theodosia, his matchmaker, his woman, if only he could convince her.* "With whom?"

"Why, you, your lordship. Was it not you who reminded me that ours should be a business relationship? You conduct business, do you not, here at the club?"

Albemarle glanced around the room. Two footmen were standing in the door, watching him carefully. Some gentlemen had already disappeared into newspapers, but most watched avidly.

Damnit, but she was bold. Bold, and brash, and determined, just like him.

His perfect match.

But this could not continue. He had to take back control, somehow, of this conversation. Even if she did make him physically weak at the knees.

"Yes, I suppose so," he assented. "Well, what business do you have in mind?"

"You are not going to allow this?"

Albemarle looked over at Braedon's horrified look. "I beg your pardon?"

The viscount was looking between them, intrigue starting to suffuse across his face. "Well…she is a lady. This is Boodle's. 'Tis not allowed."

Albemarle shrugged. "Theodosia—Miss Ashbrooke has a point. I mean, damnation Braedon, she works for a living, far more than you or I ever have. How can the woman conduct business if she cannot meet with clients?" It was only then that he realized the way he spoke at the club was probably not suitable for the ears of ladies. "No offense meant, Miss Ashbrooke."

She smiled with sparkling eyes. "Far be it for me to interrupt you, your lordship."

Was it his imagination, or was her chest heaving a little more than normal? Perhaps Miss Ashbrooke was more nervous than she was letting on.

His spirits lifted. She had come all this way, pushed herself far beyond her comfort zone, dressed herself to the nines…*all to see him.*

Miss Theodosia Ashbrooke would be the talk of the town within minutes, and she knew that. Knowing that, she came anyway.

What did she want?

"I have given greater consideration to your suggested match," she said quietly.

The flash of understanding between them occurred in an instant.

Albemarle smiled. "I believe the woman in question, in my opinion, is the perfect match for me. In every way. You are yet to argue me away from that position."

She was wily. So, she had come here to discuss his proposal, and in a way that no one else could guess. Yes, the gossips of Bath would have even more to discuss tomorrow morning. Was the Earl of Lenskeyn close to marriage?

"You must see how impossible it is," Theodosia said, her gaze not wavering from his. "Even if you wish it, the lady herself must be convinced."

Before Albemarle could formulate an answer, Braedon spoke up. "Christ alive—begging your pardon, Miss Ashbrooke—but do you mean to say you have found a suitable candidate after all! Who is she? Goodness, could you find one for me?"

Albemarle glared, but it was nothing to the glacial disdain Theodosia subjected him with.

"If you are looking for a wife, you will need to book an appointment," she said coldly, reaching into her reticule and placing a card before him. "But you must see, your lordship, that your suggestion is most irregular."

"Irregularity has never bothered me before," Albemarle said with a smile, leaning back in his chair. "When I have made up my mind, I have made it."

Theodosia lowered her voice as chatter in the room started to grow. "Even if the lady in question might…might want to consider your offer, you must see she cannot."

As Albemarle lowered his voice in turn, he carefully placed his hand on hers. "I 'must see'? Damn 'must.' I only see things the way I want, and they are not the way I want at the moment."

Was that his pulse quickening, or her own?

"You think you can convince her?" Theodosia spoke with a smile, and it was that smile that pushed Albemarle over the edge.

Damn this confining space, and damn their restrained conversation. It was time to speak openly.

Rising smartly, he said briskly, "Walk with me."

"But what about our game?" came the plaintive cry from Braedon.

Devonshire merely smiled. "Oh, let him be, Braedon," he said easily. "Can't you see the man's in love?"

Albemarle chose to ignore the comment for now but file it away for later consideration. He had no comprehension of what these sensations were. He felt for Theodosia...well, something different.

"I find I am at leisure," said Theodosia as she rose elegantly from her seat. "And you, my Lord Braedon, can write to me at that address and request a place on my rotation if you truly seek matrimony."

Braedon's mouth fell open as she swept past him. "I-I—mean—Lenskeyn!"

His cry went unheeded. It was all Albemarle could do to keep up with Theodosia as she strode through the adjoining chamber, to more shouts and cries of, "A woman! Here! Again?" and down the stairs to the hallway.

"I trust, your lordship," said the master of the club pointedly as they passed his desk, "that this will not happen again?"

Albemarle had no chance to reply as Theodosia marched through the door and onto the street. Dark, cool, and calming night air struck him as he followed her, the club's stuffiness disappearing immediately as the evening swallowed him.

Despite the late hour, there were still plenty of people on the streets. Hack drivers with their horses, sellers of drink and meat pies, gentlemen heading home from the club, ladies being escorted home from parties. It was a difficult job, weaving their way through them all.

It was plain to see by the slump of Theodosia's shoulders that she had finally relaxed after leaving the club, and yet still, she kept walking. He fell into step with her, enjoying the silence between them, feeling the closeness without needing to speak.

After a few minutes, she sighed. "I suppose I should apologize."

"I never thought you had it in you," he replied quietly.

Theodosia glared, but then her expression softened. "I did not either, but I have seen the lengths some ladies go to speak to the man they—"

"Refuse," he interrupted.

Even in the dark, Albemarle could see her cheeks pink. *Damn and blast it, man. Why can't you hold yourself together! She came to find you. That ought to mean something.*

He pulled her down a side street. It was just as dark, but with fewer pedestrians. Now they could feel truly alone.

"I meant what I said, by the way." Albemarle hated the nonchalance in his tone but had to maintain it. He could not reveal just how desperately he wanted this conversation to go well. How much he needed her.

"What you said?"

These words had to be said face to face. Her eyes were sparkling in the little moonlight of the evening, and there was that lurch again.

He nodded and stopped walking. "I want to marry you."

Was that all he could manage? One of the most important questions of his life, and he wasn't even able to form a damn sentence?

Theodosia's mouth had fallen open. "Albemarle, I am your matchmaker!"

"So make a match," he said sincerely. *If only he could find the right words...* "Match with me!"

"I-I cannot," she stammered, but he could see the hesitation in her eyes. She wanted him.

"I think you *will* not. I think you are determined not to fail at matching me," he said desperately, "but blast it all, you already have!"

"You think—when you say..." Theodosia swallowed and looked fierce. "You do not know what you are asking me. Your mother paid me to—"

Albemarle resorted to the one way he knew he could show his true feelings. He kissed her, loving the scent of her hair, the softness of her neck as he stroked it, her lips, tender and yet passionate…

He gloried in her, and in the desire that poured between them, forbidden, both knowing they should not want it, but both desperate for it.

Eventually, he pulled away.

Theodosia had a most intriguing look on her face as she whispered, "Albemarle."

His stomach lurched. "Please, Theodosia. Marry me."

"Y-You are in earnest? You an earl, and I, only a mere miss?"

"You think I care about that?" he said softly. "I see the woman you are. I see the woman I want. Marry me."

For what felt like an eternity, she was silent. And then, "Let me think about it—no, listen!"

He had not been able to prevent the groan of frustration.

"You cannot expect me to just make a decision like that."

His arms were tightly around her, keeping her close to him, her breasts pushed up against his chest in a way that made Albemarle grateful his breeches weren't fitted. *By God, but what he wanted to do to her…*

"Good enough for now," he whispered, kissing her just underneath her ear. She quivered in his arms. "But I do not think there are many young ladies in town that would have to consider marriage to an earl."

Knowing what he would want to do if they remained here, he released her with great reluctance and started walking back to the main road.

But he could not. Theodosia had kept a hold of his hand, and as she pulled him back toward her, she murmured, "And just where do you think you are going?"

CHAPTER ELEVEN

THEODOSIA TASTED THE nervousness in her throat. *Could she be completely wrong about this?*

Her gut instinct had seen her through her whole life. Never was it more important than when matchmaking. Would a gentleman of this temperament suit this particular miss? Could a miss of this family find peace with a member of that family?

Each time she had weighed up each side, carefully considered the possibilities, and then gone with her very first instinct. It had never let her down. She had never been wrong before.

Except that one time. Theodosia swallowed, seated comfortably in her armchair by the fire, and tried to push that particular situation from her mind. *Least dwelt on, soonest mended.*

But the pain from that period of her life threatened to intrude as she watched the sun go down.

Was she about to make the same mistake again? Had she learned from that reckless moment of her youth, or was she damned to repeat it, taken in once again by a handsome smile and pretty words?

"I do not think there are many young ladies in town that would have to consider marriage to an earl."

A smile curled on her lips as she rose to her feet. Anything to try to shift the pain from her heart—but then, Albemarle was making new memories with her.

Scandalous memories. Memories respectable ladies, especially matchmakers, should certainly not be creating!

Her smile grew as she sat on a sofa, nearer the window. The dark evening sky prevented her from seeing a thing outside, but just being closer gave her the illusion that she could.

Albemarle was different. Different from the gentleman she matched—or had ever met. When he spoke, it was impossible not to believe his words.

He was not a liar, nor a dissembler. He was rude, perhaps, blunt. Direct. But never false.

Why, he had no reason to lie! He was a gentleman of the realm, a peer of England, with more money than he knew what to do with. He had nothing to hide, no shame to feel, and no sense of inferiority no matter who else was in the room.

Theodosia's smile faded. How unlike her.

"I do not want a bride. I do not want a wife. I do not want children running around me. I do not want to make a home with anyone."

He had said those very words when they had first met. He had been direct from the beginning.

No other gentleman she had ever met had been so blunt. His opinion had been against marriage, and now, what a change!

Was Albemarle Howard, Earl of Lenskeyn, swept up in the power of love—or was he just a very changeable man? She had only known him for…what, a month? How could she be sure she had the measure of him?

All she wanted was to be happy. The last two days had been spent hard at work, smoothing the path for happy couples, and they had been utterly devoid of Albemarle.

They had been awful.

A knock came at the door. Her heart jumped and then started to flutter. Footsteps down the corridor, her maid opening the door—a low male voice, and the door closing again.

Theodosia's hands were in the way—but what did one do with one's hands? By the sides of her legs? In her lap? Nothing felt natural, and she needed to decide quickly because there were two pairs of footsteps in the corridor now, and it had to be him, it just had to be.

She had sent an invitation. He had not replied, of course. It was so very like him not to bother with society's niceties—but she had assumed he would attend. *If it was not him…if it was someone else, at this hour, coming to beg her help with another marriage…*

The door opened with a snap, and there stood Albemarle. He had attired himself in very smart clothes, a top hat on his head, and though he was smiling, he looked nervous.

Theodosia rose. This had been what she wanted—him, here, outside of their matchmaking, training, and formal conversation.

So why was her heart thundering so hard, she could hardly speak?

"Thank you, Robins, that will be all."

Her maid, hovering behind Albemarle with wide eyes, nodded and bobbed a curtsey before she closed the door behind him.

They were alone.

Albemarle looked around the room curiously, a smile creeping over his face.

"What is that smile for?"

"I have attempted to picture your rooms here several times, but I admit to having found the task a struggle. From what I understand, few people have ever been invited to the famous 'Theo's house.'"

She laughed. "Oh goodness, do not call me that."

"Better than Dosia," he quipped, his grin widening.

"Now, you sit down and behave yourself," she said severely, her smile still intact. "Even though this is…well, a personal visit, that does not mean I am going to accept such cheek."

Albemarle did not reply but threw himself onto a sofa and lounged back, looking instantly at ease in a way that only a wealthy, titled gentleman could.

How on earth did he manage it? Here she was, working hard to train gentlemen like Mr. Birch, desperate to gain a few more societal polishes, and Albemarle was born to it. Maybe there was something in the blood of earls.

It was certainly not something that came naturally to a mere gentleman's daughter, but Theodosia had worked hard on that particular skill years ago. She could now portray that comfort level as well as anyone—even if she did not feel it.

Seating herself at a respectable distance from Albemarle on an entirely different sofa, she sighed. "Nicknames can be a troublesome thing when you are named Theodosia. My...my parents called me Teddy."

It was strange. Admitting this familial secret felt...well, *vulnerable.* Exposed.

"I like it. It suits you well. I am surprised I did not consider it myself. May...may I call you that?"

His voice was a little stilted, almost hesitant. It was most unlike him, and Theodosia was astonished that he had bothered to ask permission. Other people's opinions had never mattered much to him before.

She nodded, not trusting her own voice. Nothing moved, save a log shifting in the grate, throwing up sparks.

They were nothing to the sparks between them, even in the silence. His presence was like a furnace, one that heated her even from a long distance. She felt drawn to him, desperate for more heat, more than she could take, until his contact could brand her.

She could never consider another man after this. No matter what happened, no matter how this ended. There was something special between herself and Albemarle Howard.

Teddy. She longed to hear it on his lips and knew that once she did, it would be a special pact between them, a moment she had shared with no one else.

She already felt, in some strange way, bound to him. And yet, not nearly as connected to him as she would like to be.

"Teddy," Albemarle whispered.

His tone caused a deep blush to stain her cheeks, and in that instant, she knew.

She loved him. The earl that had spent the last ten years on another continent. The earl who was hardly welcome in some quarters of society due to his penchant for rubbing people up the wrong way, usually on purpose.

None of that mattered. The more time she spent with him, the more endearing those traits—previously so hideous to her, so despised in society—had become.

Theodosia had spent over a decade conforming closely to society's expectations, and whenever not doing it herself, she was actively encouraging others to do so.

Conform, conform, conform. Be quiet, smile more, agree with whatever the gentleman said. Nod, agree, never make a fuss.

Matches had been made, and happy marriages created, but had *she* been happy? Had she known the rush of joy that Albemarle gave her?

He was free from all those expectations. He saw society's rules and laughed at them—or ignored them completely. His freedom made her feel free, as though society had been left behind, and they created their own world.

Despite all his faults, and there were plenty of them, and despite her failed efforts to train him, she loved him. She had fallen in love with the man before any improvements had been made and now was convinced any changes would be to the detriment of his character, not the betterment.

The rush of searing affection tied her tongue, leaving them in a silence that normally would have been unbearable. But he seemed to know how her mind was rushing from one thought to another, hardly able to catch her breath as she was overwhelmed with the realization that she would do anything, give up anything, for this man.

This wild, nonsensical man.

Theodosia swallowed. She had felt this before, of course—or at least, something like it. *She was not foolish enough to make the same mistake twice, was she?*

Was it him she did not trust, or herself?

"Marry me, Theodosia," he had whispered all those days ago.

She knew what she wanted to say. The answer was on the tip of her tongue, yet she had held back—why? Fear? Concern she would be rejected?

But Albemarle had been consistent, had he not, with his praise, with his proposals?

No matter how many myriad thoughts rushed through her mind, Theodosia knew she would have to decide soon. Albemarle Howard, despite his protestations of affection, would not wait forever.

"Have—have you heard about my latest triumph?"

The words had somehow managed to leave her mouth coherently, to her relief.

"The Lymington girl? Everyone has known about that for ages, Teddy. I hope you did not invite me over here for that little tidbit of gossip."

She shook her head, reveling in her nickname on his lips. "Do not be so foolish, the Lymington engagement was announced months ago."

"Ah, so you mean the Marnion engagement?"

Theodosia did deflate a little at this. "Oh, so you have heard?"

Albemarle laughed. "Teddy, you cannot expect to keep gossip about engagements secret in Bath! You must know that—you better than anyone! Besides, why would you want to keep it a secret?"

She did not precisely know. After all, Miss Marnion had a tidy sum of five thousand pounds for her dowry, not overly much but sufficient to gain the attention of some well-to-do gentlemen, and Sir Edward Jarvis's eldest boy was a catch for anyone.

Still. She would have liked to have told him herself.

Then a smile crept over her face. "You are right. The gossips of society are often far ahead of the official announcements—but then, I would be surprised if they had already caught wind of the marriage of the Marquess of Gloucester."

Albemarle's eyes widened. "No! Even I heard the tittle-tattle about the old Marquess—he was expected to announce his engagement with that Miss Dunder, was he not?"

"Miss Darby," corrected Theodosia with a widening smile. "Yes, he was. It all fell apart, of course. Two people can rarely be relied upon to manage their own engagements. It just isn't possible for amateurs."

He laughed. "I do not know how you do it. So they are engaged, then?"

She should not have relished the words—she should have been more humble, less excited to spread more gossip about town.

But really, today had been a triumph.

"Oh, no," she said airily. "Too much water under that bridge, I am afraid. No, I will have two engagement announcements to write tomorrow morning. The Marquess of Gloucester to a Miss Frances Lloyd, and Miss Rebecca Darby to...the Marquess of Exeter. Monty's brother."

Her pronouncement was well gratified, as Albemarle's mouth fell open as he leaned forward. "The Marquess to Miss Lloyd—she who was engaged to the Duke of Orrinshire?"

"That was almost a failure of mine, you know," Theodosia admitted. She would never have owned it to another soul, but she knew she could trust Albemarle. "It had fallen apart quite spectacularly—or at least, it would have done if I had not already selected Miss Priscilla Seton as an alternative. Really, they were fortunate to have me there."

"And the Marquess of Exeter," mused Albemarle. "You know, I do not think I know him."

"Very few recognize his name, certainly, but he comes from a good family," teased Theodosia. "Would you be impressed if I told you he was the younger brother of the Duke of Devonshire?"

He shook his head, smile widening. "Nothing would surprise me about your ability to form the very best engagements for your clients."

To be sure, Theodosia was the best. There was no one else like her in society who could make matches between what felt like the impossible people—and yet...

Engagements, marriages, matches. These topics felt strange to discuss together when their own seemed so close to the surface.

"Well, yes, it is my job," she said, a little discomfited, stomach squirming.

The earl leaned back in his seat and examined her closely. "And, so, Miss Theodosia Ashbrooke orchestrates yet another engagement."

She nodded.

"Blast it all," he exploded, unable to hold in his thoughts any longer. "And what about ours? Can we announce it? Can it be the third you write tomorrow morning to send off to those damned newspapers that need to hear all the latest goings-on?"

Theodosia opened her mouth, but no words came out.

"Let's announce it," he said warmly, his voice lowering. "Let's give those gossips something to talk about."

She swallowed. Never before this moment had she known what her answer was to be. She had wondered, swung like a pendulum between a definitive decision that she would reject him and absolute certainty that she would become the Countess of Lenskeyn.

But only now did she realize it hardly mattered what she thought. Her heart had belonged to him for a while now.

She was his, and he would be hers. But she would not give him the satisfaction of surety. Not yet.

"That is a fascinating question," she said lightly, "and one that I simply cannot consider on an empty stomach. Perhaps, after dinner, I will have an answer for you."

"Christ and all the saints in his heaven!" Albemarle rose, strode across the room, and grabbed her hand, pulling her upward.

"What are you—Albemarle, where are we going?" Theodosia protested as he pulled her toward the door to the hallway."

"Dinner," he growled. "The sooner we have it, the sooner I have you."

CHAPTER TWELVE

T HEY HAD EATEN, at least Albemarle was sure they had, for his stomach felt full, and there were a few crumbs on his napkin.

What they had eaten, exactly, he could not say. A servant had brought plates in. Plates had emptied and had been taken away.

It could have been dry biscuits for all he knew. All he could do was look at Teddy.

Theodosia Ashbrooke. She would be Teddy for the rest of his life now; he could not see her any other way.

And what a view. Stunningly beautiful, especially in the warm glow of the candlelight. A true delight to be with, witty in her conversation, never cruel when sharing gossip, and every moment, he was captivated.

She was all the sustenance he needed. If he were not careful, he could waste away just looking at her. She threw back her head and laughed as he regaled her with tales from the ship that had brought him over the Channel.

"No, really? The captain surely—"

"The captain was just as surprised as we all were," Albemarle said triumphantly. "No, I promise on my honor as a gentleman…"

The minutes slipped by, marked only by the gentle chimes of a carriage clock on the sideboard. Albemarle had never felt so untethered from time like this. He had wasted time, lost time, found time….

But time with Teddy stood still. He wanted the hands of that tiny golden clock to be stopped so this evening never ended. Because when it did, he would have to make a choice—or more importantly, she would.

By God, he hoped she chose what would make them both happy.

"You are looking at me oddly."

"My apologies," he said smoothly. "I was just...well. I could not stop looking at you."

She smiled, revealing she understood completely.

"Tell me, Teddy," he said. "How is it possible you do not see how beautiful you are?"

Now her cheeks colored, and something dark and hungry stirred within him. *If only he asked the real question dancing across his mind.* She clearly had no idea how she tempted him—would tempt any man who had half a brain and just a little eyesight.

Teddy Ashbrooke was a vision, and he wanted to do wonderful things to her, but first, she would have to ask for them. He was not one of those cads who forced a lady past the lines she set.

No, if she wanted untold pleasure from him, she would have to beg for it.

"Beautiful? You flatterer, you should be keeping those charms for the ladies," she said, dabbing at her mouth with her napkin in a transparent attempt to hide her face.

Albemarle pushed back his chair. "You are a lady, too. Why should I not notice how beautiful you are and not tell you so?"

Teddy shook her head. "Very pretty words, Albemarle. Do not worry, I like them well enough, even if I cannot bring myself to believe them."

"You really don't know, do you?" he mused.

By God, he could not wait much longer. Surely she would not be so cruel to invite him here with no intention of making him happy—the happiest man who ever lived.

His fingers itched to reach out and touch her.

Albemarle swallowed. *Damn and blast it, but she was utterly perfect. It was a miracle he had managed to fight off temptation this long.*

"Ah, the cheese," Teddy said appreciatively as the door opened once again, and a servant came in with a tray. "My favorite part of the meal."

Albemarle raised an eyebrow as the servant placed it on the table and curtseyed her way out of the room. "The port and cheese? I would not have expected to find a lady in polite society that would know much about it. Don't the ladies leave at this point?"

Teddy grinned as she leaned forward to cut herself a piece of Wensleydale. "I suppose *ladies* usually do, but I find my love of cheese sometimes overwhelms my adherence to society's rules."

She popped it in her mouth. Albemarle found himself staring at her lips.

"Besides," she continued with a little chuckle, "if you do not mind the impertinence, I will stay here and keep you company."

"I would be bereft without you."

It was honestly spoken, but Teddy rolled her eyes.

"You still do not believe me?" he asked quietly.

Teddy finished her mouthful of cheese. Then she replied in the same low tone. "It is…it is not that I do not believe you. I know you would not lie. It is just that…well. This entire thing does not feel real. You. Me. You wanting me."

Now they were finally getting somewhere. "I am determined to have you."

"Yet, just because you want something, that does not mean you will get it," she quipped. "You may be an earl, but that does not mean you are handed what you want on a silver plate."

"I would like you on a silver plate," he growled, smiling mischievously. "Bloody hell, Teddy, how can I prove it to you? How can I describe what you do to me—what you are doing right now?"

His whole body tensed with desire, and Albemarle poured himself some port. The sweet burning liquid seared his throat.

"You ask much of me," she said.

"I ask you to marry me!" Albemarle protested. "You'll be a countess! Lounging around, eating delicious food, parties, nice gowns—"

"You think that is sufficient to sway me?"

Her words cut across him, and he fell silent. *How was it possible that she could immediately see into the heart of him, see what he was attempting to?*

"I do not deserve you," he said quietly after taking another draught of port, "but I think if you managed to step away from your matchmaker mindset for one minute, you might start to see the man before you. And he is desperate for your answer."

She looked him up and down. "You do not appear to be desperate."

Albemarle groaned. *How could he take this for one more second?* "What do I have to do to show you how I feel? Write you damned poetry?"

"My goodness," she said, cutting herself another piece of cheese. "That would be a good start."

Well, he had not expected his memorizing skills to ever actually come in useful, but...

Without taking his eyes from her, he recited:

"She walks in beauty, like the night, of cloudless climes and starry skies..."

Teddy had not moved, and her gaze had not left his. She leaned forward as though drawn to him while he recited a poem he had memorized long ago from his favorite poet, Lord Byron. He had hoped one day to woo a woman with it.

There was silence after the last word of the poem echoed around the small room. Teddy appeared to be a little breathless.

"I..." She swallowed and tried again. "That was beautiful."

"And 'tis merely a snapshot of how I feel about you," he said eagerly. "Do you understand now? How I have felt about you for days— nay, weeks!"

She nodded. Words seemed to have failed her for the first time in their acquaintance.

"Now, do not get me wrong," he continued with a wry smile. "They may not have been my words, originally—"

She laughed. "Do not concern yourself, your lordship. I know Byron when I hear him."

"I will never be able to pull the wool over your eyes, will I?"

"I hope not. I hope you will never need to."

Once again, silence fell. Albemarle could feel the pressure of it. This evening was important. He already knew it was one he would never forget—*the question was, how would it end?*

Eventually he could wait no longer. "I am in earnest. Marry me."

He almost gasped at the intensity of her look. "Let us go to the drawing room," she said.

They both rose, Albemarle's fingers tingling just at the thought of being closer to her. As she passed him to reach the door, he almost grabbed her and pulled her into his arms for the first frantic kiss of the evening—but he managed to hold back.

It was when they were in the hallway that she spoke softly, "I *might* tell you my decision."

He could stand it no longer, had waited, had desperately wanted what was forbidden, but this was too much.

He knew she wanted him, and she thought she had all the power by putting off the inevitable answer to his question of matrimony.

Patience utterly gone, Albemarle pulled Teddy back, making her gasp, and pinned her against the hallway wall.

"Might?" he whispered, looking deep into her blue eyes. "Let me give you some incentive."

His kiss was passionate, fierce, like a drowning man who had finally reached the shore. If she had resisted—pushed back, perhaps, or attempted to squirm away—he would have desisted at once. He was no cad to force his affections where they were not wanted.

But they were certainly wanted. Teddy melted into his arms, returning his kisses almost more fiercely than he worshiped her.

All thought of discovery disappeared from his mind. They were the only two people in the world. They could do what they liked here, be authentic because this was the best thing he had ever done.

This was *right*. If only he could make her see, they were perfect for each other.

The thought made him pull away, and he looked down at her.

"W-What?" she managed to breathe. "Why have we stopped?"

Albemarle grinned wickedly. Despite all his finer thoughts, he would need to ensure the house was empty before he proceeded.

"Your maid," he whispered. "Your cook, any other servants. Where are they?"

Teddy stared uncomprehendingly. "You cannot possibly want anything right—"

"When do they leave, or do they live in?"

Unsure why he asked the question, she tilted her head to one side before answering. "They live out. I only have Amy Robins and a cook, and both have gone home. Why?"

Excitement soared. "Because I am going to show you exactly what you are missing by refusing to answer me, and I want no interruptions."

Slowly, he lowered his hand down her body, almost groaning aloud at the way her breasts heaved as he touched them until he reached her skirts. Inch by inch, he gathered them up in one hand, revealing her ankles, calves, knees...

"Wh-What are you doing?"

"You can tell me to stop at any time," he said quietly. "I will not force you to do anything you are uncomfortable with. But you will enjoy this, I think. If you do not, then we can stop. Trust me."

His words came out as a whisper. He could barely find the strength to speak, his whole body shaking. She was so beautiful, and he wanted her badly.

She hesitated, examining his face as though attempting to find falsehood in his eyes. Then she nodded and lifted her face to be kissed.

Albemarle lowered his mouth to hers as he moved his fingers underneath her skirts. His fingers gently brushed her thighs, and she gasped in his mouth.

He immediately stopped and broke the kiss. He did not need to speak, for she knew what he was waiting for.

"I-I..." Teddy stumbled for words. "I want you to touch me. Please."

It was all the invitation he needed. Without rushing, gently caressing and causing shivers to ripple through her body, Albemarle kissed her neck as he moved to her secret place. As slowly as he could manage, he stroked her soft opening.

"Oh!"

Stopping her cry with another kiss and trying to ignore his stiffening manhood, his fingers started to tease, caress, and then finally to enter that wet, soft place that was begging for his touch.

She was so warm, so ready for him! It took every ounce of self-control not to just unbutton his breeches and thrust into her, right against the damn wall.

"You are so beautiful," he muttered. "So very beautiful, Teddy..."

"Oh, yes," was all she could murmur, and as he kissed that soft spot just below her ear and found that delicate nub with his fingers, she shivered. "Albemarle!"

That was what pushed him over the edge. Now his fingers moved more purposefully.

He kissed her wildly, his other hand at her waist, ensuring she could not fall. As he brought her to climax, she sobbed his name, and he wondered how he would ever live without her.

She pulsed around his fingers, and he felt the ripples of pleasure moving through her until she sagged against the wall. Then she nestled into him.

"Oh, Albemarle," she spoke softly. "That was…"

His heart raced. "I love you."

Teddy smiled as though she had expected those words all along. "And I will marry you."

Such joy overwhelmed him; it was almost impossible to know what he was doing. He was kissing her again, his hands returning under her skirts and cupping her buttocks, loving that feeling of flesh—and she was hardly idle. Her fingers, unschooled but acting on instinct, attempted to undo his shirt buttons, anything to get closer to him.

"Wait, wait, Teddy," he panted, and they both ceased their frantic movements.

She looked a little abashed, as though she had been reprimanded. "You…you want me to stop?"

"Far from it. But not here."

Without waiting for a response, he swept her up in his arms and started walking upstairs.

"Second on the right," she whispered, knowing where he was taking her.

When close enough, she opened the door to her bedchamber, and Albemarle walked through it. The room was not large, with most of the space taken up by one piece of furniture.

Her bed.

With absolutely no ceremony, he placed her onto the mattress and quickly joined her, kissing her passionately as he drew her into his arms.

This was everything—she was perfection—this was the rest of his life! He never needed anything else; as long as he had her, he would feel alive.

"I love you," she murmured as he kissed down her neck and toward her breasts, almost free as he pulled at the ties of her gown. "I wanted to tell you before, but—"

"Not as much as I love you," he said intoxicated. "I love you more than life itself, Teddy, and I will always love you. I want to show you—"

Finally, his fingers were able to accomplish what he could not have done downstairs with her pinned up against the wall, and he pulled down her gown and then completely away, dropping it onto the floor.

He gazed at her. *She was not even wearing an underslip.* He had thought her beautiful before, but how could he ever countenance her wearing a gown again? She was divine, every inch of her made to perfection.

She misunderstood his groan, however. Pinking cheeks, she tried to pull at a blanket to cover herself.

"No," he said quickly. "No, Teddy…you are so perfect."

She had a nervous smile. "You…are in earnest?"

Albemarle swallowed. If he was not careful, he was going to come just looking at her, from the mere frustration of wanting her. He nodded.

"Now… you," she said a little more boldly.

He moved to the side of the bed, a little concerned his naked form would frighten her. *It had certainly been the reaction of a few ladies in the past, those far too innocent of the world.*

But Teddy did not shy away. True, he could see she was a little surprised by his manhood already standing at attention, but she quickly moved on the bed to invite him back.

Albemarle shuddered as he lay beside her. He wanted to thrust into her immediately but knew he could not. This had to be the most memorable moment she ever experienced, and for that, she needed more pleasure first.

She moved willingly into his arms, and as he caressed her, his fingers slowly coaxed another climax from her. She was so passionate that he almost came in response.

Cradling her in his arms, he whispered, "Teddy, are…are you sure about this? Are you happy to give me everything? There is no turning back once we have done this."

In response, she kissed him on the mouth, boldly teasing his lips open until she met his tongue.

Then she pulled away, her eyes blazing, "I do not want to turn back. I want to marry you. I will be your wife. Give me...give me everything. I want you, Albie."

They were the words he needed to hear. Urging her back, he kissed her as he gently entered her. As she gasped, he stopped, his free hand fondling her breasts.

"Is...is this it?" she asked. "Have we made love?"

Albemarle was careful not to laugh. *How could she know?*

"Nothing close to the end yet."

Slowly, he pulled almost out of her and then slid back in.

She was so warm, so wet, so desperate for him. She started to moan as the rhythm increased, and then suddenly, she was writhing underneath him, pulsing around his manhood, and he could hardly wait after so much wanting.

"Albie!"

Her shout was what did it. Thrusting into her harder and faster than before, he gave up trying to hold back and exploded, crying out a mixture of oaths and her name as he collapsed.

Teddy held him in her arms as he lay there, weak—*weak for her.*

Well, that was it. She had ruined him. He could never be with another woman again, never touch a woman again like this. It had to be her.

Concerned his fierce craving had hurt her, he rolled onto his back and pulled her closer.

"I love you," he murmured.

"Good," she said with a sigh. "Because I love you."

Her skin was warm against his, still tingling from their lovemaking.

"No more matchmaking."

Teddy chuckled and nestled into him. "No, not for you, at any rate."

He had to laugh at that. "What? No countess of mine is going to work! The Countess of Lenskeyn, with a job?"

Her words were drowsy now. "That is what you think…"

Albemarle glanced down and saw her eyelashes flutter as sleep came to claim her. He tightened his grip around her. *His woman. His future wife. The Countess of Lenskeyn.*

"I really do love you, you know," he whispered.

He was not sure what made him tell her again. Some part of him desperate to ensure she knew precisely how precious she was.

It did not matter, for she had already fallen asleep.

CHAPTER THIRTEEN

THE INSTANT HER eyes opened, Theodosia knew everything had changed.

The memories of last night instantly percolated through her mind.

"I really do love you, you know."

A smile drifted across her face. Every inch of her felt different, somehow. She could not have put it into words if someone had asked her. Every inch that had been touched by Albie tingled. He had teased from her body more pleasure than she had thought possible, and just when she had felt she could not take any more...

"Teddy, are...are you sure about this? You are happy to give me everything? There is no turning back once we have done this."

Her smile broadened. She was still naked, having fallen asleep in his arms. Now her sheets were tangled around her body. It was a strange feeling.

Sunlight was drifting lazily through the gap in her curtains. It was late, far later than when she usually awoke.

She would never look at the world in the same way. *How could she?* That innocence was gone. She had given it to him willingly, almost begged him to take it as her body started to awaken to the possibilities.

Experienced eyes.

She was engaged to be married—the matchmaker to the rich and noble.

It was wild! It was madness! She would be a countess.

The thought was ridiculous. If a lady had come to her with such hopes, Theodosia would have chided her gently for having such unrealistic expectations. She matched person to person, with only a little thought to title and wealth.

Albemarle Howard. He was rude, arrogant, devastatingly charming, yes. But he was also hers, all hers. He was the sort of gentleman she could never have articulated but had always wanted. *Even after that disaster with...*

Theodosia pushed the thought aside. She was not going to dwell on the past—certainly not *that* part of her past. She was leaving sadness behind where it belonged as she stepped into the happiest part of her life.

The rest of her life.

After spending so many years dedicated to the happiness of others, finding much satisfaction with seeing the joy on their faces, perhaps it was time to think of her own marriage.

More than that. Her own success.

After so much sadness, after it all going so wrong before in a way she could never have predicted, it was time something went right for her.

The last five years had been dedicated to helping others. She had so few disasters in her matches, her keen eye spotting who would make the other truly content.

How many weddings had she attended that were due to her clever work and her delicate introductions? How many engagements had almost faltered at the final hurdle, rescued by her silent intrusions?

There were even a few vicars, Lord help them, who had lost rings. Theodosia had made it a rule ever since that debacle at the Romeril wedding—which was why the mother-of-the-groom, Lady Romeril, had never quite forgiven her—that she would always carry a set of wedding rings of various sizes around with her during wedding season. They had so far been useful three times.

She smiled. You could almost call her the fairy godmother of marriages for society, and she had acted carefully and with dedication for years.

Now it was time for her to have her own happy ending.

As these thoughts overwhelmed her, whirling through her mind like autumn leaves in a gust, it was another few minutes before she realized that something was wrong.

The other side of her bed was empty.

Albemarle had gone.

A prickle of fear rushed through her heart. *Why would he leave—and without saying goodbye?* She had expected to be woken by him, and yet, here she was, the sun up, and he had left.

Theodosia rose from her bed and peeked out through the curtains. In these autumn days, it must be about eight o'clock in the morning. She was usually awake and dressed by this time, but then—and her cheeks colored at the delicious thought—*she had been kept up far later than expected.*

It would make sense, she supposed with a sinking heart, that he would leave early so others did not see him. The last thing she needed was wild speculation about her and a gentleman leaving her rooms in the early hours of the morning.

A matchmaker needed to keep her reputation or else she would lose her entire business.

She pulled on her dressing gown. It would be different when they were married. They would have their own home, their own bed-chamber. They would hide from no one that they had spent the night making love.

Her heart softened. *To think, they would have that sort of experience every night.*

A shiver rushed through her body as she crossed the room with a purpose. Her stomach was starting to protest. As she opened the door to the dining room, all she expected to find was some cold breakfast.

She did not expect to see Albemarle Howard using a dining chair to help pull on his boots.

"Albie!"

She could not help but cry out his name in relief. The happiness that swept through her as she beheld him proved last night had not been some wild dream.

As she rushed over to embrace him, Albemarle groaned. "Careful, Teddy!"

She released him immediately. "Did I hurt you?"

"Not in the slightest." He grinned, pulling on his other boot and standing up straight. "But if you touch me like that again, I will be taking you back upstairs for something I should really not be doing to my fiancée."

Theodosia smiled. It was wonderful to speak like this, as lovers, as people who would soon call each other husband and wife. "Oh, I see. And...and would that be the end of the world?"

Albie laughed, his hair falling over his eyes. "Well, no, but I would like to get a few things done today, and if you tempt me up to that bedchamber like the vixen you are, I shall get none of it completed. After all, we will be wed in two weeks."

For a moment, she was unsure whether she had heard him correctly. "Two—two weeks?"

He grinned as he stepped toward her, taking her hands in his own. "Theodosia Ashbrooke, by profession, you spend all day meeting with eligible bachelors. You think I want another gentleman taking you from me?"

His words were so ridiculous she could not help but laugh. "I think 'tis far more likely your head will be turned by another woman!"

He kissed her then, and she pulled him closer, desperate for him, her hands stroking the nape of his neck. It was a good few minutes before they released each other, which was only because they ran out of air.

"No fear—no, Teddy, I am serious. No more taking on new clients until we are married."

Still in his arms, Theodosia smiled mischievously. "You do not trust me."

He was not offended—in fact, he seemed entertained. "I do not trust myself. I am easily jealous, another fault you have yet to learn about me. The last thing I want is to be pulled up in front of the magistrate on a charge of assault."

She knew he was jesting, but still, it was rather wonderful to feel so desired. He wanted her so badly he would prevent anyone from touching her. *It was a heady idea.*

"No magistrate would ever convict you," she said aloud. *Was it possible to be this full of love and happiness?*

"Probably not. Especially not the magistrate where I live, which is where I would demand to be tried."

"Who is that?" she said, finally releasing him so he could pull on his coat.

"Why, me, of course."

She kissed him again when they reached the hallway, and he groaned as he pressed her against the wall. Wild thoughts shot through Theodosia's mind, of him pulling her into his arms again, taking her upstairs, and teaching her more ways that her body could give and receive the height of pleasure.

"Do you have to go?" she whispered as her hands moved nervously toward his manhood, which she immediately felt was hard. "Stay with me. Love me."

"Christ alive, Teddy," he moaned in her ear between kisses down her neck and toward her heaving breasts. "I want to—you do not know how badly you are tempting me!"

She laughed, fingers scrabbling for the buttons of his breeches. There was an ache growing inside her, an ache she recognized because of what he taught her.

"No—no, I mean it!" With a wrench, Albie released her and stepped back, his eyes full of desire but his hands firmly behind his back. "No, Teddy, I really must try to have some element of self-control when I am around you! If only for two weeks."

Theodosia smiled. She was starting to understand this strange power she had over him, and feeling more brazen than she had ever been in her life, and she pouted and leaned forward to allow her breasts to show.

"Really?" she breathed, not breaking eye contact. "Are you sure you cannot…warm me up before you go?"

There was a moment of electricity between them. She could almost see the sparks.

"Damn you, you tease."

In an instant, one of his hands held both of hers, pinning them above her head. She gasped as his other hand quickly moved under her skirts as his teeth raked past her breast, teasing at her nipple through her gown.

"Oh, yes," she whispered, trying to keep quiet as she knew her servants were in the building.

"Be quiet," Albie growled as his fingers entered her. "You will do what you are told."

Stopping up his mouth with a ravishing kiss, Theodosia abandoned herself to the pleasure, hips bucking against his wild and rhythmic fingers, and her mouth welcoming him in as he brought her closer, and closer, and—

"Albie!" she tried to moan, but her mouth was utterly captured by his.

He released her and fell against the opposite wall. Theodosia was unsure how she was standing, her whole body desperate to be held close to him.

She panted, "That—that was…"

"I know, and damn it, I wish my fingers had been my cock," he murmured, eyes darting down the corridor to ensure they had not been spotted. "Damn you for being so beautiful, so sweet, so delicious, Teddy. Two weeks, mark you. Two weeks, and I will have you crying out my name every hour of the day."

With that, he threw open the front door and slammed it behind him.

Theodosia leaned against the wall and was a little surprised that it did not shift under her weight.

What a man. What a life she was going to lead with him—someone who would never cease to amaze her, confuse her, surprise her.

Happiness such as she had never known was rushing through her, and not merely the physical reaction to the magic of his touch. Being loved by him was something she could never have predicted.

Despite it all, she had managed to do what she had never anticipated— she had found her perfect match.

"Did I hear the door?"

Theodosia jumped and pulled her skirts level hastily as she turned to see Robins peering around the corner curiously.

"Door?" she repeated. "No, I do not think so. Is breakfast ready, Robins, I need to depart in less than an hour."

The maid bobbed a curtsey, and soon the clatter of plates could be heard coming from the dining room. Theodosia was not entirely sure how she managed to walk the few yards to a chair, but she did, eating some hot buttered toast quickly as the clock chimed half-past eight. She would need to hurry if she were not to be late.

"Ah, Miss Ashbrooke," said Mrs. Lymington as she was ushered into their rooms just thirty minutes later. "And right on time, too. I must say I am impressed."

There were numerous clocks all chiming nine o'clock in the impressive rooms that the Lymingtons had taken for the Season. The very best rooms on Gay Street, all part of their plan to marry off their girls—and marry them off well.

"My absolute honor to be here, Mrs. Lymington," she said smoothly as they moved into an ostentatiously decorated drawing room that would make even the dowager countess raise an eyebrow. "And are we to have the pleasure of Miss Lymington's presence for our interview?"

"Sadly not," said Mrs. Lymington with a sigh as she indicated that Theodosia guest should be seated. "Tea, Dawkins. No, darling Olivia already has an engagement—such a popular child, it is so hard when one's daughter is in greater demand than oneself!"

This last sentence was said with a laugh, but Theodosia could tell as she seated herself in a comfortable settee, that there was a little sadness behind the quip.

"'Tis always the way with elegant mothers," she said aloud, in that knowing and authoritative voice that always placated the more mature women. "They raise such wonderful daughters, they simply cannot manage all the invitations they receive."

And of course, Mrs. Lymington preened, and all was well, and the appointment could begin.

"Now Miss Isabella is engaged, we must turn to her twin," Theodosia said briskly, pulling out her notebook and forcing down a yawn. "Miss Olivia. Tell me about her."

It must have been the lack of sleep. It was the only explanation for why she continued to stave off yawns over the next ten minutes as Mrs. Lymington began a monologue about the beauty and talents of her eldest born.

"—so personable, I think that is the word I would use to describe her," the devoted mother continued. "Very pretty, of course, though some have said Isabella was the prettier of the two sisters, which I have to say is very unfair, particularly when…"

Most of the words were starting to wash over Theodosia. Her notes were getting scrappier and shorter, nothing like the detailed thoughts she usually collated.

Olivia: eldest of four, twins. Younger twin engaged—to Duke of Larnwick. Pretty, personable

"—and of course, the fortune!"

Theodosia raised her head. *Yes, the Lymington fortune.* She had heard much about it through the tittle-tattle of the gossips, but she had to be sure. Such a delicate question, though.

"Yes," she said quietly. "The fortune."

Mrs. Lymington nodded impressively. "Thirty thousand! A dowry any girl would be proud of, and we have laid thirty thousand for each of our girls."

Theodosia could not help but be impressed. "That is a significant fortune."

Fortune of thirty thousand pounds.

After a moment of introspection, she underlined the last three words. She had heard no ill of Miss Olivia Lymington, and thirty thousand pounds would be enough to tempt an earl or even a duke. After all, it worked for her twin sister.

"My question to you, Miss Ashbrooke," said the matronly woman in a mock whisper, leaning toward her, "is simple. Is the earl still available?"

Something jarred in Theodosia's heart, but she managed to reply airily. "Earl, Mrs. Lymington?"

"You know the one I mean," she said, waving her hand. "The Earl of Lenskeyn. I know he is on your books, and so I ask you. Is he available?"

A smile crept over Theodosia's face, but she forced herself to be serious. "I am afraid not."

"Really? You do surprise me."

It was no surprise that Mrs. Lymington wanted an earl for her daughter. *Who would not?*

"Well, I am afraid he is not. I have heard from the best possible source he will be married in two weeks," Theodosia said as calmly as she could. *The sooner they could announce their engagement, the better.* The last thing she wanted was for her ladies to hope for her own intended.

"My goodness, I thought you were good, but I had no idea you were that good!" Mrs. Lymington had leaned back into the soft embrace of her sofa, now staring at Theodosia with an appraising air. "The Earl of Lenskeyn is notorious, as I am sure you well know, for bedding then running! You mean to tell me that he has already picked a lady—and more, that she has consented?"

A prickle of doubt, unwanted and immediately squashed, tore at Theodosia's heart. It was not a piece of gossip she had heard, but then, there would always be tales about the rich and titled of society. *Even if they were not true.*

"Well, I can assure you, he will be married within a month," she said aloud.

She was going to be happy. She had found her match, and no schemes from Mrs. Lymington, any of her daughters, or anyone else was going to take him from her.

CHAPTER FOURTEEN

ALBEMARLE ROSE STIFFLY as his mother swept into the Bath Assembly Rooms, his legs stiff and his back sore.

That would teach him. A wry smile crept over his lips as he watched his mother berate a poor footman. He was not as young as he once was, and his wild dalliance with Teddy, though delicious, had pushed his back beyond his limit.

He would have to make sure she broke him in gently.

His body twitched at the very memory of her eyes when she realized this was their future.

"Stay with me. Love me."

"And I hope you remember that!"

Albemarle sighed. Sometimes his mother was too much. She was a creature of the last century and had not adapted to the modern sensibilities of the Regent's England. She had been born in 1746 when King George II was on the throne. It had been a different country, and in some ways, she still longed for a return to those days.

"Really," the dowager muttered as she walked across the Assembly Rooms, weaving in and out of tables, "the layabouts they have for servants these days!"

Albemarle still stood by his chair. He had arrived on time and had been waiting for over twenty minutes for his mother.

The Dowager Countess of Lenskeyn had been the countess for too long to care about other people waiting for her. She was always late. It was part of being a countess.

He could remember, as though it had been yesterday—though in truth, it was almost thirty years ago—when she had taught him that valuable lesson.

"Remember, Albemarle," she had said, her parasol blocking out the blinding summer sun. "If you are always late, then everyone recognizes you as the most important person there. You are the Baron Trewessyn, and you will be the Earl of Lenskeyn one day. You will always be the most important person in any room."

He smiled and waved as she caught his eye. The Master of Ceremonies had approached her, offering her his arm.

Albemarle almost smiled as he watched heads turn to see her progress.

Always ready to make a scene. Why had she worn those damn feathers in her hat? She looked as though she was about to take a turn at a grand ball.

"I hope this is urgent," she snapped at her son as she reached the table. "I had to cancel a bridge game with the Duchess of Axwick for this, and you know how delightful she is. Far more pleasant than you."

"Hallo, Mother, 'tis good to see you."

"Hmm," was the only response he received, but she did allow him to place a kiss on her cheek as she sat down.

"I see you have gone to the trouble of ordering tea. Without me. You are an adult now, and I suppose I cannot teach you anything new, but I hope you realize how rude that is, Albemarle."

He knew his mother far too well to be offended.

"Yes, I do. And yet, I remembered how you hate tea when it is scalding hot," he said as he sat. "And so, I thought tea a little early might be the answer. This pot has been cooling these last ten minutes and should be ready to pour. Shall I, Mother?"

She glared for a moment, taking in his jovial expression.

Their table had been laid in the finest style of the Bath Assembly Rooms, one of the most prestigious locales in the whole town. Albemarle had been fortunate to secure a table at such short notice, and he had gone to great expense to ensure this conversation with his mother went well.

It had to go well. How could it go wrong?

She broke into a smile. "You know, 'tis times like this I see just what a good job I did raising you." But her smile faded as she saw the additional chair at the table. "Really, what are these people thinking?" she muttered, clicking her fingers in the air.

Within an instant, a footman appeared by her side. "Your ladyship requires assistance?"

Albemarle was impressed. *How had he managed to get so quickly across the room?*

"This chair should be removed," she said haughtily. "Or else any rapscallion might attempt to join us."

"Of course, your ladyship," bowed the footman.

Albemarle placed his hand on the back of the chair. "No. Thank you for your offer of assistance, much appreciated, but leave the chair."

The man looked between the earl and his mother, unsure who had the greater authority, but there was no shifting the chair with Albemarle's hand on it.

"Whatever you wish, your lordship—allow me to pour you some tea."

The dowager stared at her son. "Keep the chair? Whatever for?"

Albemarle smiled. *It was all coming together, his plan to make this day one of the most memorable of her life.*

"Whatever for?" he replied with a smile. "Why, where else will my future bride sit when she is to be introduced to you?"

If his mother had not been incredibly well-bred, her mouth would have fallen open.

As it was, the footman finished pouring their tea and hovered uncomfortably. "Is—is there anything else I can—"

"Of course not, go away," she said without even looking at the man. Her gaze had not left her son as she slowly smiled. "Well, well.

Four weeks! That did not take nearly as long as I thought it would."

Albemarle nodded. "I thought you would be pleased. After all your badgering, Mother, and I call it badgering for that is precisely what it was, I have acquiesced. I found the best girl, and I want you to meet her as soon as possible."

"To think, Albemarle Howard, engaged to be married," she said tartly. "I assume you have asked her, and she has agreed? I do not want some wild miss to arrive here under the impression that you are merely taking tea with her. She has expressly agreed to be your wife?"

"I do not want to turn back. I want to marry you. I will be your wife."

Albemarle nodded with a grin. "I had to propose...I think on three separate occasions. She kept saying no, for some strange reason."

His mother snorted. "Now that I can believe. What was it that finally made her agree to marry you?"

What was it that had pushed Teddy over the edge? It was wicked of him to remember the delicious things he had done to her, especially in public, but it could not merely be pleasure that had changed her mind.

No, it was his dedication, he was sure of that. He had not merely accepted defeat and then wandered off to find another woman to court.

He had been determined to have her, and have her he did.

"My charming nature," he said aloud.

It was fortunate his mother had finished sipping her tea, or else it could have been sprayed across the table.

"I am not a fool, Albemarle, and I will not be treated as one," she said stiffly. "'Tis no matter, I suppose, how you forced her into it. And was it Miss Ashbrooke who found her?"

The mention of her name made his body tingle. She would not be Miss Ashbrooke much longer, and the anticipation of his mother's reaction when she discovered that it was Teddy herself who would be the new Countess of Lenskeyn was enough to make him shiver.

"Yes," he said carefully. "Yes, it was Miss Ashbrooke who found my bride."

The dowager countess nodded appreciatively. "She is worth her weight in gold then—though I must admit, and I can tell you this now, Albemarle. Her services did cost quite a pretty penny."

"I would not worry about that," he said, trying not to smile.

"I knew it would be difficult to find someone for you," she continued, utterly ignoring him as she examined the tray of sandwiches, which had just been brought to their table. Her fingers hovered over the cucumber sandwiches indecisively. "You are just so difficult, Albemarle. You get that from me. I know that, but I needed the services of a professional to find a woman who would put up with you."

Picking up the cucumber sandwich, she raised her gaze to meet his. "She has done it then. Brava, I say. I will not be the last to thank her. I thought Miss Ashbrooke a little gruff, but she has managed to trick some poor chit into marrying you, so she cannot be foolish. Pretty, is she?"

The memory of sunlight pouring through a window and illuminating Teddy's face seared through Albemarle's mind. He thought of the way she laughed, how she raised her eyebrow when she thought he was being ridiculous...

"Yes," he said firmly. "Very."

The dowager countess sniffed. "Well, that is not everything, Albemarle, and it soon fades. I hope you will not count on it too much. Is she wealthy? Titled?"

"I..." Albemarle laughed as he opened his mouth automatically to respond but had no words.

He had no idea. They had never spoken about her family. For all he knew, Theodosia Ashbrooke had sprung out of the ground, fully formed!

It had just never seemed necessary to know. He was sure that really, as an earl, he should have requested a four-generational family history. But he did not care. She was a miss, and that was probably all he needed to know.

But wealth? Fortune? Dowry?

Money did not interest him. He had more than enough for the two of them, after all.

"You know, I have not the faintest idea," he shrugged.

"Oh, really." His mother sighed, rolling her eyes. "Trust you, Albemarle, not to pay attention to the important things! But it is no matter. Here is Miss Ashbrooke. She can tell me all about her."

Albemarle rose to his feet as his heart swelled. There indeed was Teddy, speaking to one of the footmen near the door.

It had been...what, a day since he had last seen her? Perhaps less. Twenty-two hours, but each moment without her was a loss.

Now she was coming back to him, weaving her way through the tables, and it felt like coming home. Every step she took eased the weight in his chest.

Teddy Ashbrooke. Soon to be Teddy Howard, Countess of Lenskeyn.

He bowed low as she arrived at their table. As he rose, he saw a nervous smile on her face as she glanced at his mother.

"Have you...?" Teddy's voice trailed away, evidently unsure whether to continue.

"Not yet," he said bracingly. "Here, sit yourself down."

Teddy allowed herself to be guided into her chair and glanced once again at his mother.

"Good to see you again, Miss Ashbrooke," said his mother stiffly. "Ah, young man, we require another chair."

She had accosted a footman as he passed by their table.

That excited flutter in his heart soared as Albemarle realized this was the perfect opportunity. *It was now, the moment to reveal all to his mother. He could not wait.*

"Mother, that will not be necessary."

The footman escaped as the dowager stared at her son, utterly uncomprehending. "Do not be foolish, Albemarle, of course, it is—you cannot surely be expecting your future bride to stand!"

"I do not," he said, a smile dancing across his lips.

"Albemarle," said Teddy quietly, but he ignored her.

She could not see how wonderful, how hilarious it was going to be when his mother finally realized his future bride was already sitting right before her!

"If this is the way you are going to treat your future bride, Albemarle, I will have to start thinking of ways to encourage her to stay wedded to you," his mother said tartly. "Miss Ashbrooke has worked hard to find you a bride—well done, by the way. I was a little unsure whether you would be able to manage it, to tell the truth. You can see what a difficult and disagreeable man he is."

"Mother!"

"Well, you are," she said sharply. "Still, you were recommended to be the best, Miss Ashbrooke, and you have worked a miracle."

Teddy silently implored him to intervene.

"And when is this mysterious woman to arrive?" His mother gazed around the room as though hoping to spy her. "What time did you tell her, Albemarle?"

He swallowed, excitement pouring through his veins. *This was it.*

"It does not matter," he said quietly. "She is already here."

The dowager turned, confusion across her face. "Here?"

Without replying, Albemarle reached across the table and took Teddy's hand in his. Her smile grew as he squeezed it, that reassuring pressure he could see she needed.

Then he looked at his mother, and all the color drained from his face. What had been a very funny joke—an interesting way to introduce the woman who had raised him to the woman who would raise the next generation of Lenskeyns—seemed to be going wrong.

His mother looked like she had been struck by lightning. Her face was devastatingly serious, a glare that could cut through metal.

Albemarle swallowed. It had all felt like a very clever jest when the idea had come to him. Tease his mother about his intended, have Teddy show up, and then surprise both with the announcement of their engagement.

It had only taken a few seconds to see that he had been wrong. Heart sinking, lead pouring into his heart, it was too late now.

"I forbid it." His mother's words were spoken quietly and firmly.

"I am of age," Albemarle snapped, his temper rising to the surface almost immediately. He could feel Teddy's hand attempt to pull away from his, but he kept a close hold. "Almost double the age of independence, I think you'll find."

He had done it now. He would be no gentleman if he could not face the consequences.

"You cannot forbid me to do anything," he continued. "I love her. I love Theodosia, Mother, and I have proposed to her—several times, in fact. She was quite of your mind for a while. I am going to marry her."

A medley of shock and disgust spread across his mother's face, and shame filled his own heart.

He had gravely underestimated this; he could see that now. But there was no turning back. He would not relinquish Teddy. He would fight for her with his dying breath.

"You may not have to listen to me because of your age," his mother said quietly, fury under the surface of every word, "but perhaps your respect for me, as someone much older, much wiser, and as your mother, will make you listen to me. I forbid it, do you hear me? She is—she is in trade!"

"She is a gentlewoman," Albemarle said firmly. "More—she will, by the end of two weeks, be a countess. My countess."

"She has no title, no fortune, no family, no connections!" she spat. "You think I can accept her? You think anyone in the family will accept her? You think society will expect this—this chit to become one of the greatest women of the land?"

Teddy had pulled her hand from his as Albemarle snarled, "You embarrass yourself, Mother! You think anyone will care?"

"I am going to go," came the calm words of Teddy.

His gaze shifted to her immediately. "No, Teddy. I want you to stay."

His mother sniffed at the nickname. "What nonsense!"

"I apologize, Mother, if you do not like my choice of bride," he growled, glaring. "If you recall, I had not wished to marry at all! It was you who put Theodosia Ashbrooke in my path and you who encouraged me to spend time with her to find a bride. Well, your wish is my command!"

"But—but not like this!" she spluttered.

They were attracting attention now. Heads were turning to see what all the fuss was about, and Teddy's cheeks were starting to pink.

"I have the greatest of respect for you," Albemarle said, lowering his voice. "Greater respect for you than I ever had for my father, you know that. But no amount of respect permits you to choose my bride. I have chosen her, and I have chosen well."

"This—this hoyden?"

"I love her," he said fiercely.

His mother threw up her hands in exasperation. "You cannot possibly! A matchmaker, the mother of the next Earl of Lenskeyn! A mere woman, no title, no honor, no fortune? I will not allow it."

He had not expected it to go this wrong. A quick look at Teddy told him the embarrassment he felt was nothing to the shame she was plunged into. His mother's voice, always clear and resounding, had risen with every word and was now echoing around the room. A few people furthest from them had actually risen from their seats to see what was happening.

Attempting to keep his voice calm, he said, "You can accept it or not. That is your affair. This wedding is going to happen regardless."

Unable to manage her son, she turned her fury on Teddy. "What have you done to him?"

"Me? Dear woman!" Teddy had been embarrassed, that was certain, but she was not going to permit herself to be spoken to in such a manner.

Straightening her back and giving the dowager countess just as fine a glare as she was receiving, she said imperiously, "I have done nothing to your son except push him in the direction of titled, beautiful, and wealthy young ladies. It is hardly my fault if he preferred me."

"Poppycock," his mother snapped.

"I refused your son the first two times he offered for me," Teddy said with just as much feeling, "for I, too, felt the impropriety! But I had already grown to love him, and with each passing day, the reasons to reject him disappeared. We are both adults, of age, and we know what we want."

"I know precisely what you want, you harlot," said the older woman, spite pouring from her lips. "You want a title, a fortune, a place in society your meager father was never able to give you! You have used your wiles to ensnare my son, to—"

"And is that not what every woman does, use her wiles?" Albemarle interrupted, attempting to bring some levity to the conversation. *This was all getting far too serious, too personal.*

Teddy rose. "I see no point in continuing this discussion. Thank you for your time, your ladyship."

She started to walk away.

Standing up himself, Albemarle said stiffly to his mother, "Your invitation will come by post. We will be glad to see you there, but the wedding will go ahead if you decide to stand by your foolish principles."

As he walked away, he heard her shout, "Albemarle! Albemarle, you come back here this minute and—"

It was at that point that her cries fell out of earshot, for he was too busy striding forward to find Teddy. *He needed to talk to her. He needed to explain.*

CHAPTER FIFTEEN

THE ONLY SOUND Theodosia could make out was the pounding of blood in her ears.

There must have been other sounds, of course. She could see plates being cleared away by footmen, mutterings and whisperings as people stared, even a few gasping at the way she pushed past someone to keep moving.

But she had to get away. *Far away from her.*

With no thought to where she was going, no attention paid to her footsteps, Theodosia almost stumbled as she clattered through the entrance to the Assembly Rooms.

"Mind out, miss!" a gentleman shouted as she pushed past him, no regard for politeness or etiquette.

All she was focused on was putting as much space between her and the dowager countess.

Why did it hurt so much?

She should have known. After everything she had been through, she should have predicted this would be the response. She had been foolish to think otherwise.

Blinking in the brightness of Bath winter sun, she half walked, half staggered down the street.

"I know precisely what you want, you harlot."

Theodosia could taste blood. She had bitten her lip at the mere memory of those words. *Hearing those insults hurled at her, in public, for a second time...*

It was agony. She should never have allowed herself to be put in that situation—Albie should never have done that. *What had he been thinking?*

"Theodosia!"

Her name. Someone was shouting it, but she was not interested in speaking to anyone. All she wanted to do was walk, retreat, get as far away from the scene as possible.

"Theodosia, wait!"

It was Albie. A small spark of temptation flared in her heart, begging her to stop and speak to him.

She pushed it aside forcefully as she turned a corner. If she spoke with him, no matter what he said, she knew the tears only just held back would flow.

The last thing she wanted, in this day of nightmares, was for him to see just how much his mother had hurt her.

"Teddy, stop!"

He grabbed her arm, but Theodosia wrenched herself free as she turned on him.

"Leave me alone!"

Albie stared. "And why in God's name would I want to do that? Just leave you? Ignore my mother. I always do."

"How can I?" Theodosia managed to say. Her tongue felt like lead, heavy and useless in her mouth. "I should have listened to my instincts. How—how could you let me be subjected to that? I should have rejected you outright the first time you put this ridiculous idea in my head."

"Ridiculous—what?" he laughed, his jollity grating on her spirts as he kept pace with her as she started walking again. "Instincts? I do not want to hear a single more word about your instincts against me. That is all in the past now. Teddy, we are getting married!"

But Theodosia shook her head. *Getting married? Was the man a fool? Had he listened to a single word of the conversation in there?*

"I should have refused the account as soon as I realized what you were like," she said as they paced quickly around the Circus. "I choose my clients, and in this situation, I should have said no. To both you and your mother."

The words poured from her, boiling, as though saying them aloud would remove the pain from her soul. But they did nothing but burn her mouth and lash him, the one person she should have been clinging to.

It had been eight years since she had spoken her mind like this. Well, perhaps she should have done so long ago. Maybe then, all this pent-up rage and fury would not be pouring down onto Albemarle Howard's head.

Theodosia saw the hurt in his eyes but could not stop herself. If she shared the pain, ensured he felt some of her agony, too, then perhaps she would feel it less.

"I don't know what has got into you!" Albie sounded genuinely hurt as they turned the corner. "Teddy, wait!"

"Do not call me that," she said angrily.

It was happening again. It was exactly the same as before, when—

No. She would not think of that. She would not think of *him*. She had promised herself, all those years ago, that he would not have power over her.

"I am not my mother, Theodosia, and I would appreciate it if you would not treat me like her!"

Albie's words were full of pain, disappointment, and frustration at his mother. If Theodosia had not been so full of anger, perhaps she would have heard his tone and realized that she was not the only injured party.

"Your mother is correct about one thing, though," she said. "I will give her that. You need someone with a title. With money, with connections, with—"

"Stop," he spoke the word heavily and paired it with grabbing her around the waist, forcing her to stop walking.

"Albemarle!"

This was wrong, anyone could see! But the whole of society knew she was his matchmaker, Theodosia thought bitterly. They will chalk this up to merely a tiff between a man and his servant. They would never look at her and see a bride.

"You have better connections than anyone in society, so don't talk rubbish," he said, low into her ear. "And what is more, and far more important, I know I could have someone else. I want you."

Theodosia colored. His words—although pleasant to hear—could not reach her heart. She had drawn up the drawbridge, and it would be impossible for anyone to reach it now without heavy cannons and a long siege.

His dark eyes were focused on hers, and Theodosia swallowed. He was so handsome, so kind. He made her feel…well. *Everything.* Everything she had shut out of her life. Everything she thought was forbidden. Someone destined never to be the bride, but always at the bride's side.

"You speak harshly to me, Teddy, and for no good reason as far as I can see," he murmured so no one could hear. "This feels like an overreaction. What did my mother do other than speak her mind? She is entitled to her own wrong opinion, I suppose, which is an end to it. I am marrying you."

It was impossible that they would marry. She should have seen that right from the start, and now…

Now she had given him everything and received nothing in return. The most precious part of her just been handed over, as though it was worthless, and he had taken it willingly.

"The Earl of Lenskeyn is notorious, as I am sure you well know, for bedding then running!"

Her heart hardened once more, and Theodosia attempted to observe him without being swayed by the dashingly handsome visage.

This man to whom she had initially pledged her heart…what did she know of him, really?

His title, to be sure. The fourteenth Earl of Lenskeyn was known at least by name to anyone in polite society who hoped to move in its upper echelons.

But more than that?

Nothing. A few weeks and hours together—more than any of her clients. But she had not fallen in love with any of them. She had met more eligible gentlemen in the last few years than most young ladies ever met in their lives.

So, what made him different, special?

Albie smiled. "There you go," he said, removing his arm. "I knew I could make you see reason."

The words were enough to rile her, but it was his cavalier attitude that caused fear to grow in her heart.

Her silence, her introspection, seemed to be enough to appease him. Was that all he wanted, a wife who would be quiet, keep concerns and fears to herself?

Doubt flowed in. "I wonder…"

He waited, and Theodosia swallowed. *These words, once spoken, could not be taken back.*

"I wonder whether you chose me, of all the ladies who would have loved to be your bride, because it would bring the most grief to your mother."

There. They were out.

Theodosia knew they would not be well-received. What she did not expect was him to swear loudly in the middle of Gay Street.

"How can you think that of me?" he finished, glaring with genuine hurt. "You of all people?"

The man she knew would never have thought to upset his mother in such a way—*but then, how much did she really know him?*

Most of her ladies made engagements within months. It was typical of today's society, and Theodosia had never seen anything wrong with it before. Even when a few had expressed, quietly of course, that they were a little concerned things were rushed, Theodosia had always reassured them that these things happened quickly.

Where love was involved, or even just a passing fancy that could lead to deep affection, one had to act quickly.

But Albemarle? She had accused him of merely choosing her to spite his only family, and he…

He had not denied it.

Beginning to walk once more toward her rooms, she said quietly. "I should have believed my instincts. I should have paid more attention to my notes. You are rude, Albemarle, you are arrogant, you are self-centered, and you love to cause trouble."

He had kept pace with her every step down the street, his long legs easily outpacing her own. "Perhaps, but can I not also be loving, caring, and devoted to you? Is it so strange that a man could be both?"

It was such a surprising response that she stopped in her tracks. *How could she unpick her feelings for him when they were so entangled, so mixed in her heart?*

Despite the cooling breeze, Theodosia still felt hot. His mother's words, spoken only a few minutes ago, were still ringing in her ears.

"What do you want?" Albie whispered, obviously forcing down the instinct to pull her into his arms. "Marriage? A home? Me?"

Theodosia swallowed. She had always dreamed of marriage, of a man who adored her, a home they could make together, and if God willed it, children.

Children to look like them, take after them, inherit everything they created after they were gone.

But she was no fool. She had seen enough of matchmaking to know desperation for security and devotion were not sufficiently good reasons to marry.

Had she become so in love with the idea of love that she had convinced herself she loved him—and that he loved her? Had she really been so foolish to lose her virginity, her innocence, because she felt left out? How pathetic was she?

Her blue eyes met his, and her heart twisted most painfully.

No matter what he said or did, she could not deny she loved him. Her heart belonged to him, and she would never get it back. If only she could trust him to be careful with it, to take care of her as though she were a precious crystal ornament.

Easily shattered.

As she opened her mouth to tell him that, she hesitated.

Albie's eyes had been affixed to her own. But as her mind agonized over the best way to express them, his gaze shifted...

Shifted to the pretty pair of ladies walking past them on the pavement, dressed to the nines in the latest fashions.

A smile crept over his lips that had nothing to do with her.

Theodosia blanched. It was as though he had physically assaulted her, so visceral was her reaction.

Two minutes. Less! That was the length of time she had been silent as she considered her feelings for him, and even in that time, Albemarle Howard had found someone better to look at.

Nausea rushed through her stomach. *After all his fine words, was she not important enough to pay attention to? Was this conversation about whether they truly loved each other so inconsequential?*

"And there, I think, I have my answer," she said coldly, stepping away from him. In some ways, it was like seeing him properly for the first time. "Please, your lordship, consider this jest of an engagement at an end. I certainly do."

Thank heavens she was only a few streets away from her rooms. Turning hurriedly, she paced quickly along the street, hoping to God that Albemarle would understand her tone and leave her be.

"Hold on a minute, there!"

He reached her far quicker than she could have imagined, but Theodosia kept her eyes straight and refused to look at him.

"Damn and blast it, Teddy. I cannot help noticing a pretty woman!"

Theodosia's skirts were flying as she moved. "We are discussing whether we should be married, a conversation I would consider very riveting, and you cannot pay attention!"

So consumed with her conversation with Albemarle, she had barely noticed she had already crossed over the road and arrived at her rooms.

Before she could open the door, Albemarle's hand was on her own, holding it back.

Without any regard for society, for the people on the street staring at this most bizarre altercation, and completely ignoring her shouts of protest, Albemarle pinned her against the door.

"Unhand me at once!" Theodosia hissed. "How—how dare you! Everyone is looking!"

And yet, it was impossible to forget that the last time he had pushed her up against something, he had teased her, tipped her over the edge to pleasure, and made her feel...*God, he had made her feel...*

Attempting to focus on what was happening in the here and now, she looked into his eyes.

She loved him. More than life itself, but not more than her own life. She had to protect herself, had to champion her own happiness, and would never undervalue herself again.

"Teddy," he growled. "You are starting to annoy me. Now you know this is all nonsense. You have got yourself het up over nothing. We marry in twelve days, and that's an end to it."

"No," Theodosia breathed, trying to ignore the stares. "No, if I am ever going to be the bride and not the matchmaker, then I need—I want, I deserve someone devoted to me. And that's not you, Albemarle."

The earl said something disgraceful under his breath that she did not entirely catch, and then he said, "I will not say I do not have a murky past. I will not say I have not dallied with others. But Teddy, I have chosen you."

Somehow, hearing it from his lips—that he had experienced the pleasures they had shared with others—made it all the worse.

She was no fool. A gentleman who knew how to please a woman

could surely have been no innocent. But today was overwhelming her.

What she would never say, but felt to her core, was that her pride had been hurt. Nothing had gone right today, and the best thing she could do was escape this madman and return to life as it had been.

A life without Albie.

Wrenching herself away from him with great difficulty, she managed to say, "I-I will send the fee back to your mother."

"I don't want the damn fee," he growled. "I want you. Christ alive, Theodosia Ashbrooke, I still want you, and you are not making this easy for me."

But his words only served to reinforce why this had all been, somehow, a terrible mistake.

She swallowed, knowing these would be the last words she ever said to him. "I hope you find someone who will marry you, as I will not. Good day."

"Teddy—"

In that instant, she managed to pull open the door and fling herself across the threshold, just closing it before Albemarle could get his foot in.

After the hustle and bustle of the street, the hallway was strangely empty.

"Theodosia!" came the muffled cry of the Earl of Lenskeyn as he hammered on the door. "Theodosia Ashbrooke, let me in!"

The door creaked in its hinges but did not open. She removed her bonnet and pelisse as though in a dream, hanging them up carefully on the hooks by the door.

"Teddy! Teddy, let me in!"

Slowly, she leaned against the door.

"You are being ridiculous!" Albemarle's voice was still muffled. "Look, I—I have to go. But I will be back. This conversation is not over, Theodosia!"

The bangs stopped.

Then, and only then, did Theodosia allow herself to cry.

CHAPTER SIXTEEN

"A ND THEN SHE closed the door, mark me, slammed the door right in my face without saying another word!"

Albemarle finished his story and fell back in his chair, looking at Abraham Fitzclarence, Viscount Braedon, and Montague Cavendish, Duke of Devonshire, for the confirmation he was sure he'd receive—that he was in the right, and Theodosia was in the wrong.

The two gentlemen stared incredulously as he nodded. "Not a word," he repeated with a shake of his head. "Would you credit it?"

They would agree with him, of course, they would. What gentleman would not? It was inconceivable what Teddy had done to him without a single thought for his feelings.

Taking a deep draught from the wine glass by his side, he waited for them to cry out in his defense, decry her behavior as shocking, and advise him on the best cause of action to make the woman see reason.

Braedon and Devonshire were sitting in comfortable armchairs in his rooms, but instead of instantly rushing to his defense, they remained silent.

"I ask you," Albemarle said, feeling a little discomforted and falling back on his old habit of filling the silence, "where did that come from! What was I supposed to think of all that?"

Yet still, the two gentlemen stayed silent until Braedon glanced at Devonshire with a frown. The latter shook his head.

"You...you cannot think that I was the one in the wrong?" Albemarle's voice was skeptical. "I am an earl, the fourteenth Earl of Lenskeyn, and I would never break my word. Where did she get all these ideas of outrage from?"

Braedon sighed heavily and looked at Devonshire, who said hastily, "Fault is a strong word, Lenskeyn. I would rarely call any man at fault, save for truly heinous acts, and this does not count. But then..."

"Not at *fault*," said Braedon darkly. "Not in those exact words."

These responses were so far from what he had expected that Albemarle found his temper starting to rise—never far away since Teddy slammed that door in his face.

His prickly emotions had continued since yesterday, and though in any other situation, he would have found his temper easy to control, at this moment, he was unable to prevent the explosion that followed.

"What in God's name was I supposed to do!"

Braedon opened his mouth, evidently thought better of it, and closed it. He was not usually one to offer words of wisdom, but it was unlike Devonshire to hold back.

"Devonshire, what think you?"

The man had married earlier in the year. If anyone could unpick the wild nonsense of women, it was him.

"I think you should have warned her your mother was...Christ, you know what I mean," said Devonshire with a wry smile. "Unlikely to agree to such a bold request. Well, not a request precisely. Statement."

"Bold?" Albemarle did not understand what he was talking about. "My intention to marry is hardly bold, 'tis what she demanded of me a month ago! It was her damned fault I was thinking of matrimony in the first place! If I'd had my way, I'd be halfway back to Greece by now."

"The point is, you could have chosen anyone," Braedon said. "Any title, any wealth. Who is this Teddy, anyway?"

Albemarle ignored this last question. Though he had invited them to his rooms to soothe him and tell him just how right he was, he was not ready for the world at large to know how he had attempted—*attempted!*—to wed the matchmaker of society.

"'Tis no matter," he said heavily. "She has no title if that's the information you're after, nor wealth as far as I know."

Devonshire shook his head. "I know your mother, and what's more, I like her. Even I know that taking a woman to her, lovely as I am sure she is, without title nor fortune was a mistake."

"Teddy is a gentlewoman—" Albemarle started hotly.

"And I am not saying she is not," Devonshire said, a little warning in his voice as he reached for his wine. "But not a lady with a capital 'L', am I right? Not even a right honorable. Just a woman, no offense, Lenskeyn."

Albemarle attempted to keep his temper, but the man was subjected to a very righteous glare.

It was easy for Devonshire. He had fallen in love, so the story went, with his best friend—and she had a title of her own, and plenty of money to boot.

How uncomplicated his life would have been if Teddy had been the same. But then, if she had a title, she would never have been a matchmaker—and so much of her character had been forged through those experiences.

He would never admit to Devonshire the man was right. Teddy's parents could have been smugglers, petty criminals, an innkeeper and his wife.

He had no idea. He had never thought to ask, so enrapt in Teddy herself. What did he care about her life before they met? It had brought her to him, and that was all that mattered.

Questions should have been asked. Conversation beyond his indifference to others and his attraction to her should have occupied him. Then, perhaps, he would not be in this damned mess.

"I know little about her life before we met," he admitted quietly. "I mean…it feels as though my own life only started when we met. I had assumed, in a strange way, that it was…was the same for her."

He was not embarrassed to share these things with relative strangers. Both Braedon and Devonshire had that strange quality so many of the aristocracy had of putting one instantly at ease.

Besides, on the Continent, gentlemen were far more expressive, sharing their thoughts and feelings far more often than the damned cold Englishman.

"If you ask me, and you have, so I shall share my opinion openly," Devonshire said quietly, "if you had wanted a better response from your mother, you should have told her separately and at home, not in public."

Albemarle's temper flared. "There is nothing wrong with Bath Assembly Rooms!"

Devonshire sighed. "You are being deliberately obstinate, man, and I would advise you to stop it if you have any thoughts of reconciling with both women. Do not be a fool. Sharing that sort of information in public is different than in private."

Albemarle did not reply but grunted as he took another swig of his wine. *He had not asked for reasonableness.*

"That way," Devonshire continued doggedly, "your mother could adjust to the idea slowly. You would never have endured such a scene, and this Teddy of yours would not have been shamed by your ridiculous antics and fallen out with you."

It sounded so simple when he said it like that—but Albemarle had been determined for the big reveal to occur in a place of beauty and style.

"You blaggard," said the duke softly. "The only person you thought about in that scenario was yourself."

Albemarle sighed heavily and dropped his head in his hands. "It is just…I thought it would be something to remember. Something for the three of us to look back on. I have so few opportunities to surprise my mother…"

"And this felt like an excellent way to do it?" Braedon's voice sounded muffled with Albemarle's head still in his hands. "Fun for you, certainly, but it doesn't sound much fun for anyone else. That poor woman, being flattened by your mother, and in public!"

Remorse poured through Albemarle's heart and pumped through his veins as the weight of what he had done crashed onto his soul.

Damn and blast it, the wrong decision again! How had he managed to get this so dammed wrong? Just when he thought he could make the two women so happy—one because he was choosing to marry, the other because he had chosen her—he had managed to destroy his relationship with each.

"You want a title, a fortune, a place in society your meager father was never able to give you! You have used your wiles to ensnare my son, to—"

The guilt in his stomach twisted, making him feel nauseous, and he looked up to see Braedon and Devonshire sharing a look. It was part disappointment, part disapproval, and it did nothing to improve Albemarle's mood.

This was all his fault. He was only angry at Teddy because he could not accept he had made a catastrophic mistake.

He had spent more time dwelling on how hilarious it would be, tricking his mother into thinking Teddy was there to tell her about the woman he would marry, and then revealing it was Teddy all along.

Hardly a second had been spent on thinking about how his mother or Teddy would feel.

His mother...to be told something so radical! That a servant, in her eyes, would take her place as Countess of Lenskeyn. It would be insupportable to her; he should have seen that.

And Teddy—oh, he was a cruel man indeed. To be presented with his mother, in that sort of mood, and in public! Unable to defend herself against the force of nature that the dowager countess was...

"Life never used to be this complicated," he muttered, unable to form his thoughts into anything more coherent.

He had expected...well, not comfort and solace exactly, but a little more understanding from his new friends.

Braedon laughed dryly. "It always was, I am afraid to tell you, but you just hid from it! Lenskeyn, I hate to be the one to tell you this, but you have not engaged with real life for years, almost a decade! Damnit, man, we should not be making your acquaintance properly this Season. We should have been friends for years."

"You have been playing about on the Continent, keeping away from English society," said Devonshire a little more seriously. "One cannot avoid the game of life and then complain when starting halfway through that you do not understand the rules."

"Besides, the rules have changed in the last few years," added Braedon with a sly smile. "Trust me—'tis far more complicated now to find, wed, and bed the woman you like. Or even respect! Take it from a bachelor!"

Albemarle was a little intrigued to hear the frustration in the man's tones. Braedon had experienced more than his fair share of disappointment.

But he could not think about that right now. *He had to untangle his own mess before he started attempting to help anyone with theirs!*

Devonshire sighed heavily, rose from his seat, and poured Albemarle another glass of wine. "Look, we are not unfeeling to your plight. Tell us who this Teddy is, and we may be able to offer more insight. There are countless ladies in Bath, you must know that."

Albemarle swallowed. Keeping Teddy to himself had felt like the right thing to do. He was certain she would not want the news of their failed engagement to become known in society.

The gossips of Bath would have plenty of fodder if they heard the matchmaker had attempted to wed the Earl of Lenskeyn.

But as Albemarle glanced up at his guests, he could see that he could trust them. These were men of honor and probably had secrets they would rather keep out of the gossip columns.

They would understand.

"Theodosia," he said heavily. When neither of them changed their expressions, he grinned wryly, "Yes, not many people know her

Christian name, but she is the matchmaker around here."

Understanding dawned. Devonshire leaned back in his chair and whistled slowly. Braedon chuckled and shook his head as though a great joke had been made.

"Well, that explains a great deal," Devonshire said with wide eyes. "A girl in trade, Lenskeyn! No wonder your mother almost exploded."

"A matchmaker! *The* matchmaker?" said Braedon with a giggle. "Wasn't she supposed to be finding you a bride?"

Albemarle nodded, unable to speak.

"Well, she certainly succeeded!" Braedon said. "Christ and all His saints, you have got yourself in a pickle."

"The trouble is you fell in love with someone whose job, whose very position in society is to help others fall in love," said Devonshire musingly. "She has probably never felt the emotion herself, so 'tis all new to her."

Albemarle shifted slightly in his seat. *This sounded like it was leading somewhere that would be uncomfortable.* "And?"

Devonshire rolled his eyes. "Damnit, man, maybe you are simply not ready for a bride. She was frightened!"

"Frightened?" Albemarle stared, utterly uncomprehending. *Where was this man going with this nonsense?*

"She knows you are a rascal—even if she did not hear it on the gossip, you probably showed her countless times. Despite that, despite the differences in your positions, despite the very situation in which you were introduced, you managed to get her to promise something— herself. Not a small commitment for any woman."

"And then," chimed in Braedon, taking up the tale, "it all seemed to be slipping away, and worse, *she* was blamed for getting her claws in *you!* I certainly would not want to face your mother once in a temper, no offense meant, and you gave her no warning."

Devonshire sighed. "I have heard she is a woman who can fend for herself, but no one, not even Miss Theodosia Ashbrooke, should have to face your mother."

Was it possible for him to feel more wretched? Albemarle wanted to drop his head into his hands and block out the world. He had thought himself so smart, and yet all he had managed to do was hurt everyone around him.

"Wait…Miss Theodosia Ashbrooke. Ashbrooke, you say?"

Braedon's words made Albemarle look up. The viscount appeared concerned.

"Yes," Albemarle said. "What of her?"

Albemarle's heart fluttered.

"What do you know of her?" he said a little insistently. "Out with it, Braedon!"

The younger man swallowed, and the panic growing in Albemarle's chest increased. There was something about Theodosia Ashbrooke that he did not know, and based on Braedon's hesitancy, it was not good.

Damn and blast it; he should have asked more questions! They had always discussed him, never her. What was she hiding?

"Look," said Braedon hastily, "it is all gossip, you understand me? I was not there myself, and I did not hear it from anyone who was."

"Bloody Nora, just tell me!" Albemarle did not attempt to keep his voice calm, frustration from the day before pouring out. He sighed and tried to collect himself. "I apologize, Braedon. I should not have shouted. But God's teeth, you are testing my patience. Out with it!"

Braedon sighed heavily again. "You were not in London then. Probably on the Continent, and the news would never have reached you—I mean, why would it? You did not know her. You had no passing acquaintance with anyone involved. There is no reason you would—"

"Braedon, if you do not get a move on, I think Lenskeyn will hurt you," Devonshire said with a wry smile. "Get on with it."

Albemarle leaned forward. "Come on, man, tell me all. I am ready for anything. What is it—secrets? A scandal?"

The youngest of them then said slowly, "Only you could make it sound sensational when really, it was just the same old story we have heard time and time again. A gentleman who called himself the Earl of Cragmore was in town and this Miss Ashbrooke was probably only about…oh, I don't know. One and twenty?"

"Eight years ago," said Albemarle quickly. "Yes, I was in Germany. I would never have met the Earl of Cragmore."

"You never would have," said Braedon darkly.

"I never met him either, you know," Devonshire said slowly. "Why didn't I have a passing acquaintance with—oh, eight years ago? I was on my Grand Tour, never mind."

"Well, this Earl of Cragmore was in town, and so was Miss Ashbrooke, and things progressed as one would expect," Braedon continued quickly now, eager to get the words out and his story over with. "He proposed marriage, and she accepted. They started planning the wedding, and it was all going swimmingly. Until…"

His voice trailed away, and he gulped at his wine, seeming to need the liquor to continue.

Albemarle's heart was slamming against his ribcage. *Teddy, engaged to another man? Another earl, if that could be believed!*

She had never seemed like a widowed woman. She had never mentioned it in all their conversations, but then, fool that he was, he had never thought to ask.

He knew so little of her. Only now was he starting to realize it.

"Well," said Braedon, looking distinctly uncomfortable. "One hardly likes to spread gossip about a lady—"

"What is the point in starting a story if you are not going to continue!" Albemarle snapped. His nerves were pushed to the very edge of what they could take. He had to know.

What had happened to Teddy?

Braedon sighed. "I only heard it from others, mark me so that I may have some of the details a little wrong, but this is what I know. Only a few days before the wedding, the man's mother caught them up."

"The dowager countess," said Devonshire softly.

But Braedon was shaking his head. "No. No, she was just a Mrs. someone, a Right Honorable, something."

Albemarle was unable to take in the meaning of the viscount's words. "How does a Right Honorable lady's son become an earl?"

"Christ, your woman has done a number on you," Braedon said with something of his old cheerfulness. "You don't understand, do you? The man was not the Earl of Cragmore. He was not the earl of anything. He had no title of his own, no money, and his mother had tracked him down after a previous scam had gone awry."

Something seemed to be awry with Albemarle's ears. *What he had just heard could not possibly be right.*

"What?" Devonshire said, his voice harsh. "The blaggard!"

Braedon nodded. "What's more, this Miss Ashbrooke wanted to continue the marriage."

"What?" It was the only syllable that Albemarle could manage, but its fury summed up his feelings.

"I heard she said that she loved the man, not the title, nor the expectation of wealth and consequence," Braedon said heavily. "But the man's mother would have none of it. She didn't consider Miss Ashbrooke good enough for her son, even though he wasn't the man he purported to be. And the fool was swayed by his mother and disappeared from London overnight."

Albemarle's heart, previously thumping so wildly, seemed to have stopped.

"This false earl and his mother disappeared, never to be seen again," Braedon said. "Miss Ashbrooke was left to pick up the pieces—and the bills from the wedding plans already made."

Albemarle could not speak. Thoughts were swirling in his mind so rapidly that he could barely hold one of them long enough to understand it.

Teddy, abandoned—Teddy, believing she was engaged to an earl, finding he was not who he said he was.

And if that wasn't bad enough, the mother then turned up, forbade the marriage anyway, and whisked away the man she loved.

Oh, Christ.

"She had to start working to pay off the debts incurred in planning the wedding," said Braedon in a brittle voice. "Bills her future husband would have paid if he had been the man he said he was. She has been a matchmaker ever since."

Albemarle's mind rebelled from what he was hearing. *It could not be true—it was not possible. People simply did not act that way!*

But he had seen enough of humanity to know that was precisely how some people acted.

Perhaps Braedon was lying. It was a terrible tale...but then, why would he lie?

Teddy, engaged to a man she had thought was an earl. She had believed in him, fallen in love with him, been proposed to, accepted him, planned a wedding with him—a life with him!

And then the mother arrived to drag him away, break the affection between them.

Oh, God in his heaven.

"I did not know," he said hoarsely, his voice cracking.

"'Tis a most unfortunate coincidence," said Devonshire delicately.

Albemarle laughed darkly. "And, of course, my mother attempts to forbid our marriage!"

Braedon nodded. "No wonder your Miss Ashbrooke reacted the way she did. It must have brought up quite a few painful memories, those shenanigans you forced her through."

Albemarle rose from his seat, unable to stay in it as his restless feet moved up around his rooms like a caged lion.

"How in God's name am I going to make this right?"

CHAPTER SEVENTEEN

THEODOSIA BLINKED, AND her notes came swimming back into view.

Rebecca—beautiful, born 17—friends with…lately connected to…greatest skills are:

The individual words made sense, but together they were meaningless. *What had she been attempting to write? What had she meant?*

She swallowed, tasting the bitterness in her n throat. Two nights with barely any sleep had done nothing for her ability to concentrate. If she had been paying more attention, her notes would be better.

"—three years ago, and last year there was an almost dalliance with a gentleman by the name of—"

Embarrassment curled around her heart, but there was nothing for it. If she had been paying attention, she would not need to say this.

"I do apologize, Lady Cramer," she said quietly, and the stately woman halted in her tracks. "There is…well, so much information about your charming daughter, I am struggling to jot it all down. I need to return to your thoughts about your daughter's greatest skills."

Lady Cramer looked down her nose and sniffed, clearly affronted. "Return? Why, that was five minutes ago!"

There was something rather unique about being stared at by a woman with a title who knew herself to be superior. It was like being examined by a large animal. They were not going to pounce. *They did not need to pounce to prove they could hurt you.*

The room, full of marble and silence, was still. Lady Cramer had requested a visit to the her rooms, but Theodosia had made that mistake only once. Never again.

So they were seated in the stifling drawing room of the Cramers. The lady of the house was being slowly enveloped by the softest sofa Theodosia had ever seen, while she had been offered a stool.

A wooden stool.

"Well?" said Lady Cramer into the silence. "Did you run out of pencil?"

"Yes—yes, my pencil," Theodosia grasped at the excuse with relief. "My pencil has become blunt. There are so many things to note about Lady Rebecca. I would greatly appreciate it if—"

"Benjamin!"

Theodosia's words were interrupted by a shriek from Lady Cramer. Immediately the door opened, and a footman walked in, bowed, approached his mistress, and bowed again.

"My lady?" he said quietly.

"The matchmaker requires another pencil," Lady Cramer said imperiously as Theodosia carefully hid her pencil in her reticule. The last thing she wanted was for them to see it was perfectly sharpened. "A pencil for the matchmaker."

The footman bowed, and the two ladies were left in uncomfortable silence.

In any other one of her appointments, Theodosia would have attempted to break the silence. It was always easier to find a match for a lady or a gentleman, for that matter, if one had a good understanding of the parents.

One did not always become one's mother, Theodosia knew, but it was a taste of things to come.

Lady Cramer, on the other hand, was formidable. There was nothing in particular that Theodosia could attest to it, for she was not sharply spoken; she was not cruel; she was not rude.

But there was a coldness there. Something that made Theodosia shiver.

It was little wonder her daughter, Lady Rebecca, was eager to be married. And after that scandal with Edward Wynn, that viscount—well, it had been *almost* hushed up.

A not quite hushed-up scandal was liable to leave a lady, no matter her title or wealth, on the shelf.

The door opened once more, and the footman returned, carrying—Theodosia saw with a sinking heart—three pencils, carefully sharpened, on a silver platter.

She swallowed. It was a deliberate choice to make her feel inferior, and it was well done. But she had spent enough time with ladies of all dignities and titles to know that it was not personal.

At least, not to Theodosia. Just to all ladies who had not married a marquess or higher.

"Thank you," she said to Lady Cramer rather than the footman, as society expected. "That is most kind of you."

Graciously taking all three pencils from the silver tray, she placed two on the table beside her and poised one above the paper in her notebook.

"So, your daughter, Lady Cramer. Her talents."

Just as many ladies did, in Theodosia's experience, Lady Cramer immediately preened. "Well, of course, Lady Rebecca is rather like me in every regard, so we may find we do not have sufficient room in that little notebook of yours!"

Theodosia smiled automatically. *Every mother felt the same about her daughter.* It was one of life's little rules, which eventually became grating.

"Of course," she said aloud. "We will have to see when my pages run out! I will, naturally, summarize for my notes."

Lady Cramer tried to look at the matchmaker's notes so far. Theodosia leaned back ever so slightly to ensure her nonsense could not be read. *Even upside down.*

"Beauty, naturally," Lady Cramer snapped, thoroughly irritated she had been unable to peek. "A fine wit, too, only the other day Lady Romeril was telling me…"

Theodosia tried. She really did. Concentrating as hard as she could, with every intention of writing it all down faithfully, the pencil worked quickly across the page.

After all, this was not only Lady Cramer, wife of the Marquess of Pembroke, but a new client. There were six daughters in this family. If Theodosia could make a good impression for the first, the other five could find their way onto her books—and their fees into her purse.

Ladies, ladies, she was always on the hunt for ladies. One would think it would be the other way around, of course, but in fact, it was often the gentlemen who were desperate to find the right match.

Not just the right lady, but the right family, the right fortune, someone to be mother to their heirs.

As her pencil scratched across her notebook, her mind was frequently interrupted by thoughts of that…*that damned man.*

She was allowed to curse, after all, if silently.

"I don't want the damn fee. I want you. Christ alive, Theodosia Ashbrooke, I still want you, and you are not making this easy for me."

Theodosia pushed the thought away. She had to concentrate—if she asked Lady Cramer to repeat herself a third time, she could say goodbye to Lady Rebecca as a client, or any of the Cramer girls.

"—plenty of admirers have noted on that," Lady Cramer was continuing. Her nose scrunched up. "I will own that my daughter has had a fair number of potential suitors. None, of course, who have lived up to the standard her father and I would want for her."

Theodosia nodded. "I quite understand, Lady Cramer."

Yes, she understood better than almost anyone what it was like to not quite live up to the expectations of a mother.

"I know precisely what you want, you harlot."

She forced a smile. She would not dwell on the past. She would move forward. She had always managed to make her way through the world.

"It is imperative, I feel, to find someone of the right caliber," Theodosia continued, giving that little speech that always placated exacting parents. "Marriage is for life, after all, and it is not merely between a gentleman and a lady, but their families. If the families are not well-suited, it matters not what connection the couple themselves have. The families must be matched just as carefully as the gentleman."

For the first time in their interview, Lady Cramer smiled. "I am so glad you understand, Miss Ashbrooke. Believe it or not, my Rebecca took a little time to come to my way of thinking."

It did not surprise Theodosia at all, though she made some murmurs of surprise. No, today, there were plenty of daughters who were starting to discover that they had opinions, and their desires, and their wishes for their own lives. It was taking the older generation a little while to absorb this.

"Now when it comes to the gentleman in question, a title of course," Lady Cramer continued. "We cannot have our eldest daughter married to a nobody. Even a viscount would be preferable to a mere *esquire*."

She spoke the word as though it tasted foul.

"A good income would be advantageous, but a house both in town and the country is what, I believe, would make Rebecca most happy," the caring mother finished.

Theodosia nodded as she wrote in her notebook. She estimated that it was Lady Cramer who would appreciate two homes for her daughter. She looked down at her notes.

Title, viscount minimum. Good income. House in town and country.

It was impossible not to notice the description of the perfect suitor for Lady Rebecca was…well, Albemarle. Her earl.

The earl. The fourteenth Earl of Lenskeyn. She must stop considering him something of a possession of hers—he was not hers anymore.

He had never been hers to begin with, and she needed to forget him.

A small part of her, treacherous and irritating, wondered whether the best way to get rid of him, both in her heart and in reality, would be to do what her instincts forbade, introduce him to Lady Cramer's daughter. If Lady Rebecca was all her mother described, even putting aside poetic motherly license, then it would be a good match.

And that, she thought dully, *would make her the most noble matchmaker in the world.*

As though able to peek not merely into her notebook but into her mind, Lady Cramer leaned forward and spoke in a mock whisper. "I have heard a rumor that a gentleman who fits my description perfectly is on your books, Miss Ashbrooke. Of course, it may be pure speculation."

Theodosia carefully constructed a look of mild puzzlement. "My word, Lady Cramer, that would be fortunate indeed. What rumor, and about whom?"

It was too much to hope, of course, that Lady Cramer was thinking of someone utterly different. *Perhaps she had not heard about the Marquess of Exeter's engagement?*

"Do not be so modest," the older woman said with a knowing smile. "You have proved yourself to be a wonderful matchmaker for Lady Romeril's oldest boy, and I am sure if you had another specimen of that caliber—an earl, let's say—you would not keep him from me."

Her coyness was not sufficient to mask who she was referring to.

"It is very flattering to hear such good reports of my skills, and from Lady Romeril," Theodosia said placidly. "Now, Lady Rebecca. After she completed finishing school, where did—"

"The Earl of Lenskeyn, of course!" Lady Cramer's patience ran out. "I had heard he was to be married in ten days, God knows who to, which I must say you have kept very quiet! But then I heard, and from Mrs. Bryant no less, that the wedding had been called off. So is he available, Miss Ashbrooke?"

Theodosia hesitated. It would be so easy to say yes. She knew, in her heart, that the chances of marrying the earl had disappeared.

She had walked away from him, broken off the engagement, and refused to see him. The one letter that had arrived with his seal had been returned unopened.

She was not going to be marrying Albemarle Howard, the Earl of Lenskeyn.

But saying it aloud, to another person—to the mother of a client, no less—would make it all real in a completely different way.

Taking a deep breath, Theodosia closed her notebook. Her fingers brushed against something tucked in the back.

Her heart twisted. She had kept it, against her better judgment, and had not read it in all the eight years it had rested there.

She had almost thrown it out two years ago, but something had stopped her, as though it could, one day, bring her joy.

Perhaps now was the time...

Pushing aside what she was about to say, she said, "Lady Cramer, would you be so kind as to give me a moment, alone? I...I need to consider your daughter and the range of suitors that I currently have," and she lifted up her notebook, "on my books, as it were."

She could have said nothing better to excite the woman before her.

"What—that is how you make the match?" she asked excitedly. "Just like that?"

Theodosia smiled. She had never revealed her process for matchmaking and probably never would. *A magician never revealed his secrets.*

"Not entirely," she conceded. "But 'tis the first step, and can often lead to the greatest connections. And now I have the earl in mind from our conversation..."

Allowing her voice to trail away was the perfect trick. Lady

Cramer could not look more pleased and wished to strike while the iron was hot.

"Of course—I believe the fire in the breakfast room is still lit. You will be warm enough there."

Theodosia's smile was just a little brittle. Far be it from Lady Cramer to exit her room when she was so comfortably ensconced on the sofa. No, it was for Miss Ashbrooke, the matchmaker, to rise from her uncomfortable wooden stool and find her way to another room which, she was sure, would be freezing.

"How kind," she said aloud.

Lady Cramer bellowed, "Benjamin!" And the footman appeared.

"My lady?"

"Take Miss Ashbrooke to the breakfast room," said Lady Cramer. "And give her anything else she requires."

She even deigned to incline her head as Theodosia rose and curtseyed. It was a relief to step across the drawing room, down a corridor, and into the breakfast room, which had a little more cheer. Decorated in fashions from at least ten years ago, it was cozier, with less marble and a fire far warmer than she had expected.

"Anything else you need, miss?"

Theodosia shook her head. "No, thank you."

Bowing his way out of the room, the footman closed the door, and Theodosia was left alone.

Heart twisting painfully with the anticipation of what she was about to read, she sighed and stepped across the room to sit nearest the fire. Gently, taking care not to disturb the other bits of paper which she had stuffed into the notebook, the letter finally rested in her hand.

The letter from *him*.

Resting her notebook on her lap, she carefully removed the letter from its envelope, smoothed it out on the notebook, and read it.

Dearest Theo,

This is the fifth version of this letter. I may have to write a sixth. I may never even send it.

You know I cannot apologize enough. I know mere words will never be sufficient to heal the pain I have caused you, and so I say once again, I am so sorry, knowing it cannot atone for my heinous crimes.

I really do love you, more than I can ever say. More than words can express—but I was blinded by fear, that enemy of love, that taunted me saying I was not worthy of you.

Inventing the title was wrong. It was wrong, and I am sorry, and I have been punished more severely than I could have thought: by losing you.

Please do not weep for me. I do not deserve your tears, and the last thing I would wish is for you to distress yourself on my behalf.

Mourn for me, as though I had died. The gentleman you thought you knew never really existed. So much of myself was hidden from you, even as I fell in love with your innumerable excellent qualities, and so you have not lost a man to another. He has died.

Mourn me, and then like any widow, look to find love again. You are young, you are precious, and you are deserving of love.

The very last thing I would wish would be for you to distance yourself from life. Happiness, joy, connection: all these things you should seek, when you are ready.

Theo, you have so much to offer a gentleman. I would know better than anyone, I think, just how happy you can make a man, even without trying.

Besides, I know you. I know it is possible for you to completely miss out on finding the best gentleman for you because of your own stubbornness.

Please accept my apologies, consider me lost to the world forever, and when you are ready, look for love elsewhere.

I am sorry.

I am, forever, your most faithful servant,
Frederick Marsh, esquire.

Theodosia looked up, her eyes dry. Even now, reading his words, the pain returned—but it was dull.

In the silence of the room, she gasped. *She could no longer remember Fred's face.*

Looking into the flames, as though their flickering light would help jog her memory, only one face appeared.

Albemarle. His face surfaced in her mind, handsome and brilliant.

And rude, she reminded herself. *Entitled, stern, direct...*

A rueful smile crept over her face. He wanted to marry her, and she was confident that this time, he really did have a title.

Could Fred have been right? Was it possible that after the pain of her first engagement, she could miss the opportunity to be happy with Albemarle?

One thing she was sure about. She deserved to know happiness. There was nothing more emotionally exhausting than always making a match for others, seeing them find that person who would make the rest of life's struggles bearable.

Theodosia glanced down at the words of Fred again.

Theo, you have so much to offer a gentleman. I would know better than anyone, I think, just how happy you can make a man, even without trying.

It was time to make her own match.

Her fingers brushed over the signature of the first man she had ever given her heart to. *Frederick.* She had loved him so much. At least, she loved the idea of him.

Leaning forward, she allowed the letter to fall into the flames and watched until all the words were gone and the paper utterly indecipherable.

As she re-entered the drawing room, her hostess looked a little ruffled. "Miss Ashbrooke! There you are. I almost sent Benjamin out to check on you. I have been waiting."

The words were spoken pointedly, but Theodosia smiled as she sat back down—this time, on the sofa opposite Lady Cramer.

"I know," she said simply. "And so have I. The Earl of Lenskeyn is getting married in eight days."

CHAPTER EIGHTEEN

WITH A GREAT sense of triumph and more than a little pleasure, Albemarle threw down a trio of kings with a smile.

"Oh, no!" Braedon groaned, looking at the pile of silver before them. "Three kings?"

"You blaggard," said Devonshire, rather more good-naturedly. "To think, you have been huffing and puffing all this hand, and in reality—"

"He was bluffing!" chuckled Braedon.

Albemarle laughed. Cards were a great distraction from his heartache—not entirely sufficient, but useful. He knew his recent friends, Abraham Fitzclarence, Viscount Braedon, and Monty Cavendish, Duke of Devonshire, had come over for the third evening in a row to keep him company.

It was kind of them, and he felt the benefit of their friendship as he had never felt with others before. Still, not enough to force Teddy from his mind.

"I have said it before, I think I will end up saying it a thousand times," Braedon offered. "I am sure you are cheating! Are these cards marked? Do you have another pack hidden somewhere up those big earldom sleeves?"

Devonshire was still chuckling. "You only ever think others are cheating when you are losing, Braedon—almost all the time, now I come to think on it!"

The three gentlemen laughed. Braedon was smart enough to have learned to laugh at himself, Albemarle could see—a skill he had not entirely mastered himself. Living in a village in the middle of nowhere in Greece made him a fascinating figure for the locals. He was more accustomed to being adored and respected than laughed at.

Perhaps Braedon and Devonshire were good for him.

It was strange to think, had everything gone as it should have with Teddy and his mother, he would be having a very different evening.

If his foolishness had not tripped him up.

It would have been Teddy who sat opposite him, not Braedon, and instead of playing poker, they would have been planning a wedding.

Not a wedding. *Their wedding.* His wedding to the most wonderful woman in the world.

But he was gambling instead. He had more coin than he knew what to do with, and he was sufficiently adept at poker to ensure he did not lose too much.

Thankfully, their game was not accompanied by only a bottle, as it had last time. His butler, Blenkins, had sent up more than enough food to be getting on with. Half a roast chicken still sat on the sideboard, along with the vegetables that accompanied it, potatoes, gravy, and the pudding they had been unable to stomach.

"Well, I still think it's a con," said Braedon heavily as he pulled the cards toward him, ready to shuffle and deal the next hand. "And I think it most unfair of you, Lenskeyn."

Albemarle spread his arms wide. "I cannot help it if I am more skilled at cards than you, Braedon."

"Hmph!" said the viscount with a wry smile. "You know, for a gentleman who is supposed to be lovelorn, you are doing an excellent job of taking all my money."

Albemarle glanced down at the pile of coins before him. It was true. It had certainly grown in the last hour. But money? *What did he care about money?*

The one genuinely precious thing he had, he'd lost. Just when he was sure he had secured her, Theodosia Ashbrooke had stormed out of his life. And he would never recover her; he was sure of that.

After his conversation with Braedon and Devonshire, he had made some...delicate inquiries. The story Braedon had told whirled around his mind, restless, and he had to put it to bed.

A part of him had hoped it was false. Sadly, the information he received demonstrated quite the opposite. A Miss Theodosia Ashbrooke had indeed been engaged to a man who called himself the Earl of Cragmore.

Albemarle had snorted at that. There was no earldom of Cragmore, and anyone could have looked that up in Debrett's *The New Peerage.*

But Teddy had not. She had engaged herself to him, planned for their wedding, and then...the mother had arrived.

"You want a title, a fortune, a place in society your meager father was never able to give you! You have used your wiles to ensnare my son, to—"

It had all fallen apart, and so had Teddy. She had disappeared from view for a while until re-emerging into society as a matchmaker.

A loud banging just outside the house drew Albemarle's attention back into the room. "Just deal the cards, Braedon," he said smoothly.

"Happily," said the man with a grin. "I will have to if I wish to win my money back!"

Devonshire smiled. "I would not be so certain, Braedon. Lenskeyn is a better bluffer than either of us—he has the whip hand at this table."

The uproar outside was growing louder.

Albemarle ignored it. "I think it most unlikely you will win back all of it, Braedon, old boy! I'm more likely to take a few more coins from you!"

He was forced to raise his voice as the banging and clattering rose. *It almost sounded as though someone was attempting to batter down his door.*

Sighing, he leaned over and picked up a silver bell. Within a minute, his butler appeared at the door. "You rang, your lordship?"

"I did," said Albemarle quietly as Braedon dealt out the next hand.

"Do me a favor and find out what on earth the matter is, will you? That damned noise is disturbing our game."

Blenkins bowed and disappeared from the room as Braedon cried, "There, and much good may they do you!"

Albemarle shook his head with a smile as he reached for his cards. Two threes, a six, and a nine—and none of the same suit.

It did not matter. He had at least a decade of experience playing poker over the impetuous Braedon, and he had managed to bluff his way to winning with worse hands.

"Now, what does that smile mean?" Devonshire said thoughtfully.

Braedon looked up hastily. "What smile? Lenskeyn is smiling?"

Albemarle chuckled as he rearranged his cards into a completely arbitrary order. "Now, if you start to look for tells, Braedon, you are going to be disappointed. A guinea."

He threw the coin into the center of the table.

Braedon looked aghast. "You can't start the bidding at a guinea?"

"Why not?"

"Because…because…" Braedon was lost for words.

Devonshire chuckled. "You must have an incredible hand to start the bid at a guinea, Lenskeyn!"

Albemarle allowed his face to relax. *The thundering noise was still crashing about outside, but if he could just concentrate…*

"Fine. Fine!" Braedon threw down his cards. "I fold. Are you happy?"

Albemarle could not help but grin again. If he decided to stay in England, he could foresee many happy—and profitable—evenings playing cards with Braedon.

"I know what I have, and I am willing to take you to the cleaners to see what you have," he said aloud, more to Devonshire than to the viscount. "Will you match my guinea?"

Before the duke could reply, Blenkins returned and lowered his head to murmur into his master's ear. "There is a lady outside."

By pure coincidence, at that precise moment, the banging and crashing noises outside ceased, and the whisper carried far further than the butler intended.

Both of the guests laughed.

"A lady, outside! At this hour?" Braedon said, turning to look at the window as if that would reveal her identity. "How rebellious of you!"

"Well, I expect he thought we would be gone by now," said Devonshire quickly. He laughed at the confused look on his friend's face. "Old Lenskeyn probably ordered one from the nearest bawdy house and thought by this hour, we would have lost all our money!"

Albemarle smiled mechanically and glanced at the grandfather clock. It was just past nine o'clock.

Not particularly late for him, but very late for a lady to be out, and on her own?

He frowned. "Who in God's name is she, Blenkins?"

The words he so desperately wanted to hear were ones he never would. Teddy would never demean herself to come and see him.

She had made it clear she considered their engagement ended. The letter he had written, groveling, desperate, had been returned unopened. He had burnt it, as though the destruction of the letter could remove the pain.

He had last seen her almost a week ago at the Assembly Rooms with his mother.

Now neither woman was speaking to him.

In all honor, he should have been more upset about his mother. He had been refused entry to her rooms, and she would not answer his letters.

His mother on the one hand, his lover on the other. His heart was Teddy's, utterly and without strings, and he couldn't just take it back because she no longer wanted him.

Another hearty bang on his front door echoed through the room.

"Damnit, what does she want?" he snapped at his butler.

Blenkins glanced carefully at his master's guests before speaking.

After just a few weeks of serving the earl, Blenkins managed to get on with him quite nicely. The butler knew never to disagree with his master, and Albemarle knew not to take a step into the kitchen. It was an uneasy truce, but it worked.

"The lady," whispered Blenkins, "wishes to see you, your lordship."

"Goodness, she is persistent," said Devonshire with a grin. "Who do you owe money to, Lenskeyn? That sounds like the knock of someone determined to come in!"

It certainly did. The banging was starting to get genuinely irritating, and out of sheer annoyance, Albemarle snapped at his servant. "Well, let her in then, damnit, and we can get the foolish business over and done with," he said with very bad grace. "She cannot possibly make as much noise in here than out there."

"Very good, my lord," said Blenkins quietly.

"You know, you certainly lead a wild and rebellious life, Lenskeyn," said Braedon affably. "I am not sure whether I would be able to keep up! Women turning up in the middle of the night!"

"Hardly," said Albemarle dismissively. *The sooner he saw her, whoever she was, the sooner she could leave.* "And I am still waiting for Devonshire to see my guinea or fold. Devonshire?"

Albemarle watched the man carefully. There was that tell, the tugging of his left ear, that told the world that the cards in his hand were useless.

But he was intrigued, Albemarle could see that. Devonshire wanted to see what he could be throwing a guinea at, and that meant…

"You know what," he said slowly. "I think—"

"Teddy."

Albemarle had not intended to speak the word aloud. Teddy had just walked into the room, cheeks pink and pelisse wrapped tightly around her.

To someone who barely knew her, she would be unrecognizable.

No bonnet, her pelisse pulled up to her face, and her hair pulled back in the simplest hairstyle—but it was her.

Albemarle knew every inch of her intimately. *He would know her anywhere.*

"I say," said Devonshire slowly, looking between the two of them.

Braedon looked up and whistled. "My word—the girls these places send are getting far more refined than I remem—ouch!"

Although Albemarle could not be sure, it appeared Devonshire had kicked him under the table.

Teddy's cheeks, already pinkened by the night air, darkened.

"What did you do that for?" Braedon rubbed his shin with an angry look.

"I want to speak with you," said Teddy quietly, looking straight at Albemarle.

Was he dreaming? Even with the sensation of the cards between his fingers, it was difficult to believe what he was seeing was real.

Teddy—here, in his rooms, late at night! What did she think she was doing?

A part of him was so thrilled to see her; he did not care. He could look. He could spend the rest of his life just looking at her, knowing she was safe, knowing at any moment, he could reach out…

But pain played harmony to the melody of affection. Though she was before him, she did not belong to him anymore, and it was his foolishness that had lost her.

If he had just taken the care to find out about her past, ask her about her family, her time in London, anything like that…

Well, then he would have known just how upsetting his stunt at the Assembly Rooms would be.

Damnit, he did not deserve her. He wanted her, that was true, but it was not the same thing.

If he were honest with himself, and a physical wrench seemed to twist his stomach as he thought it, she would probably be happier without him.

"Albemarle?"

He stood up hastily as Teddy said his name. "Yes, yes, of course, we can talk. Let us go into the—"

"No," she cut across him quietly. "Here. Do you love me?"

How could she ask such a thing of him—and before strangers to her, too! Albemarle could see the hurt as she asked him. *The very fact that she had to ask...*

The gazes of both Braedon and Devonshire burnt his face, and it was difficult to ascertain who was the most embarrassed, himself, Teddy, or his guests.

Albemarle swallowed. The last thing he wanted was to embarrass himself by pouring out his heart before two men he only met a month ago—but he had no choice.

If he did not embarrass himself now, he would spend the rest of his life wondering.

What if? What if he had pushed himself, finally, outside his comfort zone? Instead of laughing, jesting, being sarcastic...*what if he was honest?*

Teddy needed him to make that gesture. He understood that now.

He nodded.

"I don't think I caught that," said Braedon with a grin.

Albemarle cuffed him about the head and then immediately looked back at Teddy. His heart swelled.

She was everything to him. Of course he would embarrass him-self—anything to have a second chance to win her heart.

"Yes, Ted—Theodosia," he amended hastily. "I love you."

Teddy took a step toward him. "You have never declared anything like that in your life, have you? It is time for you to be the man I know you can be. Are you sure you love me?"

"Yes," croaked Albemarle. He was not entirely sure where his voice had gone, and he coughed before saying, "Damnit, Theodosia, you know me better than anyone—you know me better than I know myself. You know how I feel about you."

"It's not enough."

Her words were soft, but they cut into Albemarle's heart like knives. "Not—not enough?"

Out of the corner of his eye, he saw Devonshire glance at Braedon.

"Well, I should be off," said the duke hastily, rising to his feet. "The wife will be wondering where I—"

"Will you love me tomorrow?" Teddy's question was simply asked. There was no guile in her voice. *This was something she needed to hear.* "Next week? Next year?"

Albemarle knew she needed far more reassurance than he could give. How could he predict the future? Yes, he loved her now. He would gamble his entire fortune that he would still love her tomorrow, and next year, certainly.

He would not live forever, but she needed to know he would love her for every instant he was on this earth.

What were the words she needed to hear?

"Yes," he said simply. "All the days of our lives."

He stepped toward her as he spoke, his fingers itching to touch her again. *It had been too long since Theodosia Ashbrooke was in his arms.*

Teddy whispered, "I am not sure if I am ready to trust you yet."

"I am sure," he said boldly, pulling her into his arms. "And you have all the time in the world to learn just how trustworthy I am."

She did not resist as he kissed her. She melted into his arms, kissing him back just as fiercely as he poured down his affection for her.

He was home. He had never felt adrift before he had met this matchmaker who teased and tantalized—but now he had her in his arms, she was the anchor of his world.

Everything he wanted in the world, everything, was in his arms at this moment.

He had never wanted a bride. He certainly had never wanted a wife.

But Teddy was not just a chit of a woman he would have to put up with. She was his perfect match, his better half, the person he wanted to love every single day.

When he finally pulled away from her, she was blushing.

Without taking his eyes from her, Albemarle barked, "Braedon? Devonshire? Out!"

He heard Devonshire laugh. "And well, you may say that, you old dog—I have just peeked at your cards! I cannot believe you were bluffing on such a terrible hand!"

"But I want the chance to win all my money back!" came Braedon's plaintive voice. "You mean to tell me you are just going to throw us out?"

"That is what I intend to do," said Albemarle, looking into Teddy's adoring eyes. "I have far more important things to do."

With much muttering and bad grace from one, and laughter from the other, the two gentlemen left the room.

It did not feel empty as the door closed behind them. On the contrary, the room now felt like theirs. *Their very own.*

Teddy smiled, still in his arms. "And what do we do now?"

Albemarle released her from his arms and grabbed her hand. "Come with me."

He had pulled her into the hallway before she asked, "But where are we going?"

Albemarle stopped in his tracks. This did not seem real. Here she was, everything forgotten, all past wrongs erased.

It did not seem right.

"Why did you forgive me?"

The question echoed in the hallway, and Teddy looked a little askance. "I...I realized you meant no harm. With your mother, I mean."

Regret pained his heart. "I cannot tell you how sorry I am that—"

"I know." Teddy looked at him closely, and her hand squeezed his. "I lost the chance of happiness once. The fault was not mine, but that did not matter. I-I lost it. Now I have the chance for happiness again, and this time, true happiness."

Albemarle did not speak. He could see how difficult it was for her, saying these things.

"One day, I will tell you all about it," she said, breathing out heavily with a laugh. "But not today. Suffice it to say that in thinking back to my past, I realized what I wanted my future to be. And it was with you. Dowager countess be damned." She ended with a wry smile.

Albemarle kissed her hand. "You know I still intend to marry you in eight days, don't you?"

"Absolutely not," Teddy said decisively.

His smile faded. "What?"

A natural smile tilted up the corners of her mouth. "I will need at least fifteen to plan this wedding, Albemarle. When I become Theodosia Howard, Countess of Lenskeyn, it is going to be the best wedding society has ever seen."

Cupping her face in his hands, Albemarle kissed her passionately, pouring out all his fears that he had lost her and the relief she had come back to him. He would never stop loving her—he would never stop showing her just how loved she was.

When he finally released her, both of them were breathless. Albemarle took her hand in his again.

"Come on."

"But—but where are we going?" she asked curiously as they started going upstairs.

Albemarle grinned. "To show you just how much I love you."

CHAPTER NINETEEN

"**Y**OU ARE MARRYING a woman with great organizational skills!" protested Theodosia as she looked up from her lists. "What on earth did you think was going to happen?"

She looked across the drawing room from the desk that Blenkins had set up for her, right in the window, and stifled a grin.

There he was. Her Albemarle, lying on a sofa with his eyes closed and hand covering them to block out the autumnal light.

"I just had no idea that weddings were so blasted complicated!" he said, not bothering to open his eyes.

Theodosia really did laugh this time, and as she did so, her stomach swooped. Placing her hands on her stomach to settle it, she swallowed down the words she wanted to say. *Today was not the time. They had far more important things to think about, after all.*

When the right time would be, she was not entirely sure. But one thing she did know, *it would be obvious.*

And so, instead of speaking the words desperate to be poured out, she said briskly, "Albemarle Howard, a wedding—nay, a marriage is a complicated thing. One cannot simply throw up one's hands and hope all the pieces come together! All things must be carefully considered, weighed, chosen, then acted on!"

Albie did not reply unless one counted a harrumph a reply.

Theodosia smiled and shook her head before turning back to the uppermost list on her desk. "So, the guest list. 'Tis almost finalized, with just a few individuals to consider. Lady Romeril, I suppose, must be invited."

A groan emanated from the sofa. "Yes, damn it. Irritating woman."

His bride-to-be frowned. "You cannot say that, Albie. True, she is a little outspoken, but perhaps the world would be a better place if more women spoke their mind."

"It is not Lady Romeril's mind I have an issue with," came the muffled reply. "It is her inability to keep that mind out of other people's business!"

"Nevertheless, she is a stalwart of society."

"A buttress, you mean."

"I will add Lady Romeril to the list, then," Theodosia said, forcing down another laugh. *Really, she would have to watch herself. Marriage to Albie was going to make her more cutting in her remarks if she was not careful.* "Now, I have a 'Lady Howard.' One of your relations, I assume? Great-aunt?"

"Sister-in-law. Widow of Elmore."

"Oh, that Lady Howard," said Theodosia, a little crestfallen. Now she had found Albie—and had put their differences and misunderstandings behind them—it was devastating to think of losing him. *And Elmore had been the younger Howard brother...*

She turned around to look at her future husband. "We must have her, then."

"Poor Elmore, he should have lived," Albie said, lifting up his hand to look at her. "Yes, Lady Howard should be there. We have to have her, in fact, because there are rumors she may be with child."

Theodosia turned away quickly. "Really?"

"I don't know how much credence to give the gossip, but there is a chance."

Her heart was beating faster, but she was able to keep her voice calm as she said, "From what little I have seen of her, she was—what would you say, one and thirty?"

"Something like that," came the unconcerned voice of Albie.

"Time will tell, I suppose. No, we must have her."

"One and thirty. No age at all to be a widow—at least, not for long," mused Theodosia, reaching for her notebook. "I wonder whether she would appreciate a conversation with a matchmaker…"

Opening up the notebook, she added a note to her list of potential ladies as Blenkins came into the room, white gloves on his hands, to check on the silver in the sideboard.

Lady Elmore Howard—widow. One and thirty. With child?

"Damn you, Teddy, no wife of mine is going to keep working!"

As Theodosia turned around, she saw her protective fiancée had sat up and was glaring in a most attractive way.

She gave him her most brilliant smile. *Really, he was too marvelous for words.* The way he wanted to protect her, give her the best the world had to offer.

"I absolutely am," she said, turning back to add Lady Elmore Howard to the growing guest list. "And no husband of mine is going to attempt to change my mind. It would be a foolish errand to be sure, and you have much better things to be getting on with."

She heard him shift on the sofa.

"You know, I think I shall have to have a word with that young Braedon," she said lightly. "Keeping you out at all hours. What time was it that you returned here last night?"

There was no response—at least, no verbal response. A long, low groan echoed around the room.

"And all those bottles," Theodosia teased. "Blenkins told me this morning that all the wine he had accumulated for your cellar has mysteriously disappeared."

Blenkins glanced at her with a harried expression at the exact same moment that Albie sat up, looking outraged.

"Mysteriously disappeared!" he protested. "All I did was take a few bottles to my friend's, and why—"

"Miss Ashbrooke, I had no cause for complaint!" Blenkins interrupted as he glanced nervously at his master. "I merely wished to discuss for the wedding—"

Their voices were overrun with laughter. "Do not concern yourselves, either of you," Theodosia said. "I merely wish to point out, Albie, that perhaps one's headache would not be quite so bad if you did not keep taking bottles over to Braedon's for his card parties. A viscount should provide his own refreshments."

He smiled wryly. "Well, perhaps. Is that another one of your society rules?"

Theodosia turned back to her guest list. *There were still so many people to review.* "Yes, I think so."

"I suppose I should not be surprised," came the cheeky response as Blenkins left the room, evidently mortified. "You called me arrogant when we first met—"

"And a great number of times subsequently," Theodosia added absentmindedly.

"But I think that quality is more alike to determinedness, and you have that in spades."

She could not help but smile. It was true. The more she had grown to know him, the more she had realized just how alike they were.

She did not reply immediately. *The guest list was too long—or was it?* How numerous were the guests at an earl's wedding? She had never planned one before. *Not really.*

"I should have noticed we were each other's perfect match within days," she said with a smile as she crossed off Mr. Lister. *There was no chance of him coming to her wedding.* Not after his behavior toward Tabitha Chesworth—now the Duchess of Axwick.

"Perhaps your skills are slipping?"

Theodosia shook her head. "No, if anything, they are now more astute. All the more reason to continue with my matchmaking services—yes, Albie, continue! I have so many people still on my books, and it would be most discourteous to simply give up on them. At least for the next six months or so."

She could not help but see whether her words had been understood.

Her hint, however, was utterly ignored. Albie still had his hand over his eyes, and as she watched, he sighed heavily.

Theodosia shook her head. Albemarle Howard was very clever in some ways, remarkably intelligent even. But in some ways, he was as ignorant as a child.

As though able to feel her gaze upon him, Albie removed his hand and grinned. "Are you finished? I want my bride back, and I have lost her to that damned organization. Surely there cannot be more to do?"

Theodosia glanced at the lists spreading across the desk, the few that had slipped onto the floor, and the others left on an armchair as part of tomorrow's work.

"At the current rate we are going?" she said lightly. "I would say...three days."

Albie laughed and tried to speak at the same time, causing him to splutter. "Thr-Three days! Goodness, Teddy! Far be it from me to criticize, but aren't we getting married in five?"

"We are," she said serenely.

"I think my mother and a few other guests may get annoyed if we postpone," mused Albie, "and I certainly would hate to be kept from your bedchamber any longer."

A curl of anticipation made Theodosia shiver. It had been incredibly difficult keeping Albie's hands from her this last week. *Now, more than ever, she wanted the comfort of his touch—but no.* She had told him, repeatedly, that he would have to wait until he married her.

She was going to stick to that one, no matter how tempted she was.

Albie sighed into the silence. "I suppose we could postpone if we really had to."

"I would not recommend it," Theodosia said. "The sooner, the better."

Should she say more? Was it fair to leave him in the dark? How could he be expected to make decisions for the next few months if he did not know?

"I suppose you are right. So many of these blasted plans made already," Albie said, leaning back into the cushions of the sofa. "I can only imagine how complicated it would become, attempting to rearrange them all. Even you, mistress of all organization, would probably be hard-pressed to do it. No, I should probably leave you alone to get the damned lists finished."

His eyes closed, and he sighed heavily.

It was all Theodosia could do not to laugh. *Really, it was most provoking! Was this the right opportunity, then, to tell him?* She had wanted to the last couple of days, but then it was difficult to know when the perfect moment was.

Once the truth was out, there was no taking it back.

Looking at him made her stomach swoop and her heartbeat quicken. She loved him so much. She wanted to give him everything, everything in the world. To be his bride was one of the greatest honors of her life.

His bride, and then...

With a sudden spurt of energy, Albie sat up. "You know—I am hungry. This damned hangover needs curing, and I do not think the hair of the dog would be advisable. Blenkins has had almost nothing to do these last few days. You eat so little. What would you like? They can make anything for you—if ingredients are not to be found here, one of the maids can go out."

Theodosia turned back to her lists. "No, thank you."

As she continued to scribble down a few notes for which of her guests should not be permitted more than two glasses of liquor, there was silence.

Then Albie's voice rose, concern in every tone. "Are...are you sure? You have not eaten anything all morning."

"I am not hungry, thank you," she said, glad she had her back to him. *It would not do for him to see the pink dots on her cheeks.*

"You should eat, you know," he continued. "Your mind needs sustenance if it is going to untangle the damned seating chart. What has happened to your appetite, anyway? You never used to send back food or decline cake. Cake! You!"

Theodosia's pencil stopped. *Trust Albie not to notice anything except she had ceased eating cake!*

It was now. *Now* was the moment. She was unlikely to have a better one, just the two of them together, and if she were not careful, even Albie's ridiculous ability to ignore what was before him would cease.

Surely, he could not be that stupid.

Placing her pencil down on the desk and tidying her lists together, she turned to look at the man she loved.

"Albie," she said quietly. "I will probably not be eating most mornings. Not for a little while."

Theodosia had been sure that statement would be enough. He was older than her, after all. He had seen so much more of the world, met so many different people.

Albie rolled his eyes. "Teddy, I cannot believe I am saying this, but you will fit into your wedding gown fine. Please do not worry, and please, for love of all things holy, do not miss meals."

"No, 'tis not that," Theodosia began.

"I have no desire for a slip of a wife anyway," Albie continued, shaking his head seriously. "I want a real woman that I can grab hold of in the bedroom."

He smiled wickedly, and she almost laughed. *Really, but there was no shifting his mind once he picked up an idea.*

Rising from her seat and fighting the nausea that immediately swelled as she walked across the room, she pushed his feet onto the floor to make room for herself on the sofa.

"No, it is not that," she repeated softly. "It is just that I do not wish to eat in the mornings—and some afternoons, too. I feel too unwell."

The teasing joy in his face immediately disappeared. "Unwell?" His eyes raked over her, taking in her pale complexion. "I will call the doctor. Doctor Sanders will—"

"Albie," she interrupted, almost laughing. His concern was so endearing.

His expression filled her with such hope, it was challenging to think of the words to speak.

"Please, Albie, there is no need," she said placatingly, putting a hand on his arm. "I have already consulted Doctor Sanders, and everything will be fine. He is not concerned in the slightest, and neither should you be."

Albie's eyes narrowed slightly. "So...so you are sick, but he is going to make you better? Do you need any medicine? Christ alive, Teddy, I have left all the wedding planning to you, and here you are, telling me that you have been feeling so unwell you have consulted a doctor!"

"No, please do not concern yourself with—"

"I am the most selfish creature that ever lived," he said thoughtfully. "I always have been. But I will improve, Teddy, I promise."

He was the most endearing man.

"I love you the way you are," she said, attempting to reassure him. "Please—"

"No more lists," he interrupted most emphatically. "Death by lists, I knew it! Hand over all that damned paperwork, and I will see if I can make head or tail of it."

Theodosia was so full of happiness; it was almost impossible for her to speak. But she must.

"The doctor said," she began slowly, "I will start to feel better after three months, then it is three months of feeling quite normal, and then three months of staying at home and doing very little. And then..."

Her voice trailed away. The words to describe what would happen next simply did not come.

Color drained from his face. "Not...not consumption? Teddy, darling, you aren't trying to tell me that—"

"No, no, of course not!" she said hastily, taking his hand in her own. "No, after that..."

Albie swallowed. His fear appeared to prevent him from speaking, but he finally managed to say, "Then you will be better?"

Theodosia squeezed his hand. "Then I will have a baby."

There was a moment—and she had no idea how long it was, but it seemed to tip into eternity—when Albie just stared. His dark eyes met hers and did not let them go. His breathing seemed to stop, and his face became expressionless.

Theodosia found that she was holding her breath, too. *There. It was said.* Now she would see whether he was interested in having a family, or...

She was pulled quickly into his arms as he cried, "Teddy!"

His passionate kiss prevented her from speaking as he gripped her tightly, and then he pushed her back, his hands on her arms, as his gaze searched her wildly as though looking for clues of the child.

"You—you are sure? My God, a baby—a child! Are you sure? A family already?"

Her laughter was part excitement, part relief. *He was happy!* He was happy, he loved her, and he was going to be the most incredible father.

"As sure as I can be!" she laughed. "I missed my flux. I am tender. I have morning sickness... Doctor Sanders agrees with me that it is most likely I...I am with child."

"With child," Albie whispered, his grin not fading. "A baby girl! Or boy, I suppose—is there any way to tell?"

Theodosia shook her head. "There are certainly plenty of old wives' tales to predict what our little one will be, but I think waiting will be half the excitement."

"A baby," he said, almost in awe. "I cannot believe it. Well, I suppose there was always the chance—we were not careful. A family! And here I was, just six weeks ago, despising the idea of a *bride*."

A hint of concern tinged Theodosia's happiness. "Then...then you do not mind? I could be wrong, of course, and even if I am with child, there is no guarantee the pregnancy will go smoothly and—"

Albie interrupted her with a kiss. Theodosia accepted it willingly, pouring out her fears, her desperation to be close to him, clutching at him as though he were the only real thing in the world.

At that moment, he was.

When he finally released her, she had all the reassurance she needed.

"I want you, and I want this baby," he said. "We are a family. Even if it isn't this time round, then it will be another time. And even if it doesn't happen at all, I have you, Teddy. *You* are the woman I fell in love with."

He kissed her again, swiftly, and Theodosia smiled, feeling tears prickle at the corners of her eyes. "I love you, Albie."

He sighed heavily. "Damnit, I wish we could be married this afternoon."

Theodosia smiled. "Not without finishing my lists."

EPILOGUE

THEODOSIA ASHBROOKE WAS utterly alone, gazing at her reflection in the looking glass. She wore an elegant gown, tucked under the bosom in the popular empire line style, in soft white muslin. Embroidery at the sleeves and hem gave the gown a richness that suited its purpose.

Today was her wedding day.

The room felt strangely empty as she chose the earbobs she would wear as she became Lady Theodosia Howard. No bridesmaids had been chosen. Friendships required time, and she had rarely had much time of her own. Every moment had been spent matching others.

Any lady who appealed to her sense of humor, tastes, and character had usually become acquainted with her as a client. Theodosia's nose curled at the very thought of it.

One did not befriend a client.

But then, and a wry smile crept over her face at the thought, *one did not marry clients either, and she was about to do just that.*

"Damnit, I wish we could be married this afternoon."

Her wry smile softened. She was marrying the best man she had ever met, and that was saying something. Little had she known what would befall her when she approached the dowager countess at the Orrinshire wedding.

There were moments when she did not entirely understand how she had managed to catch him. One small misunderstanding, one decision which led to pain that had threatened to part them forever. She had been hurt before and had been determined never to be hurt again.

But all that was behind her. Today, and all the days that followed, she was going to be happy.

A church bell rang out across Bath, chiming eleven o'clock. In just a short hour, she would become a countess—the Countess of Lenskeyn, and her heart fluttered, and her stomach, already unruly, swooped with joy. She would be Albie's wife.

Theodosia placed a hand on her stomach and smiled. It was only nausea for now, but in a few months, she would feel a flutter of movement.

A family. A family she would love for the rest of her life.

Taking a deep breath and ensuring her appearance was sufficiently bridal, Theodosia turned and left her bedchamber for the last time. As she walked down the stairs, her maid peered up from the hallway.

"Oh, miss, you look lovely!"

Theodosia smiled. "Thank you, Robins. You will ensure all our belongings are taken to—"

"Miss," interrupted the servant with a smile. "Do you not have more important things to consider, such as your lateness? Here is your posy. I'll be the one crying at the back of the church, miss."

It was impossible not to smile as she accepted the small bouquet and stepped out onto the street. Despite the late autumn day, the sun was bright and brilliant against a pale blue sky.

The street was packed, as Bath always was, and some stared at her.

It was Mrs. Lymington, however, who accosted her as she walked down Gay Street. "My word, Miss Ashbrooke, you look...well, lovely!"

Theodosia tried to smile. *How like Mrs. Lymington to be unable to give even the briefest of compliments without a hint of disapproval.*

"And where are you off to?"

Before she could reply, Mrs. Lymington was speaking again.

"Now, I have no wish to detain you, Miss Ashbrooke, I can walk along with you for a little way," said the woman with a frown, as though Theodosia was doing her a great disservice by not stopping. "I have not heard anything from you about a potential match for my daughter. 'Tis most vexing."

Theodosia almost laughed as they continued down the street. It was, really, a fitting way for her to walk to the church. *To think, she was going to be harassed as a matchmaker, even on her own wedding day!*

"Mrs. Lymington," she said calmly and politely, "I will be happy to help you in a few days, but first, I have to go to my wedding."

The hint was not subtle, yet Mrs. Lymington ignored it. "I know you have many weddings to attend, you make so many matches, but I want to attend my daughters' weddings myself, and if you do not hurry up, then I will not be able to!"

Theodosia's smile only grew. They had almost reached the church now; she could see its gates. "I understand your concerns, I assure you," she said quietly, "but I need to be getting to my wedding. I will call on you in a few weeks, Mrs. Lymington."

They had reached the church now, its bells peeling and flowers adorning the archway of the door.

Mrs. Lymington looked up distractedly at the church. "Whose wedding did you say it was?"

With an intense sensation of pleasure, Theodosia smiled. "My own."

As she walked down the aisle, slowly and alone, faces jumped out from the congregation: her successes.

There was Charles and Priscilla, Duke and Duchess of Orrinshire, perhaps her most notorious success. There was Lieutenant Perry and his wife, married a few years since and with a babe in arms. The Needhams were there, too, almost an entire pew filled with their offspring.

Her heart swelled. She had been crucial for their happiness, giving her great joy in the past—but nothing like what she was experiencing now.

This was her story, and it was not the end but the beginning of a new chapter.

Albemarle Howard, fourteenth Earl of Lenskeyn, was waiting for her at the top of the aisle.

True, it was not the earl she had originally thought she would marry, but Albemarle was a better man than Fred had ever been. He was wild, demanding, irritating, rude, and in every situation sought to tease her. Despite her best efforts, she had not managed to train Albie away from his worst habits—but she did not care.

Theodosia loved him, bad habits and all. If this experience had taught her anything, it was that she might need to rethink that part of her matchmaking business.

At last, she reached him and placed her posy of flowers onto the pew to her left.

"At last," Albie whispered. "I thought you would never get here."

Theodosia smiled. "Honestly, neither did I."

There was a hearty sniff behind her. Turning, she saw the dowager countess, staring with an imperious look, making it clear she had still not forgiven the matchmaker for stealing away her son.

Theodosia inclined her head politely at the matriarch of the family she was about to join and turned back to Albie and the vicar, who smiled.

"Dearly beloved," he began. "We are gathered here today…"

The wedding flew by so quickly that she was barely able to keep up. *How many weddings had she attended—tens of them? Perhaps a hundred?*

And yet, during her own, it was impossible to pay attention. All she could take in was Albie smiling and promising to devote his life to her.

"—do declare them man and wife."

Albie's fingers had entwined with hers, and he squeezed them as the vicar pronounced them as married.

"Hello, wife," he whispered.

Before Theodosia could think of a reply, the service was over, and they were walking out of the church, flowers soaring over their heads as cheers went up outside.

Albie swept her into his arms as soon as they stepped over the threshold of the church and kissed her passionately. She returned his ardor, clinging to the man who made her so happy.

They broke apart as scattered applause and muttering gasps finally reached their ears.

"I love you, wife," Albie whispered.

Theodosia smiled. "I love you, husband."

"And," he continued in an even lower voice, "I love our child, even before she arrives."

She laughed as he finally released her, and they clambered into the carriage waiting for them. It was only a twenty-minute carriage ride to Lenskeyn House, the country house just outside Bath—one of their country houses. He had reminded her last week.

"She? You—you cannot possibly know what it is. And don't you want a son?"

Albie shook his head as the carriage rattled across cobblestones. "Son? Heirs? All that nonsense never bothered me. 'Tis my darling mother who panics about an heir, and much good may it do her. I just want a family—a family with you."

Theodosia could think of no better reply than to kiss him most heartily—and indeed, they could have easily spent hours in that carriage, kissing and whispering sweet nothings to each other. They were married, and they were happy, and they would be for the rest of their lives.

Upon arrival at Lenskeyn House, a whirlwind of guests who simply had to share their congratulations with the happy couple descended upon them.

"You know," Theodosia whispered to her husband during a lull in hand wringing and kisses on cheeks, "I will be glad to get off my feet."

Albie smiled sadly. "Not yet. There is still one last guest we need to welcome."

Taking her by the hand, he approached a woman who had hung back.

Theodosia's heart sank. It was Lady Howard, evidently trying to keep a smile on her face.

She had never given much thought to widows and widowers. Now she had Albie, and it was impossible to imagine losing him.

But that was what had happened to Lady Howard. After five years of a marriage that was, by all accounts, happy, she had lost him—and had no children to comfort her in her time of grief.

"Lady Howard," Albie said kindly.

Lady Howard smiled wanly. "Congratulations on your marriage, your lordship, Lady Howard."

"We are honored that you came," said Theodosia quietly. *What else could she say?*

"I wanted to," she said quietly. "And I also wanted to…to give you this."

There was a wooden box in her hands, about the same size as those tea caddies that were becoming quite popular. She handed it to Theodosia, who opened the lid curiously.

Dazzling sparkles hit her eyes. Diamonds. Jewels, rings, a string of pearls, a brooch that looked heavier than all her jewelry put together…

Theodosia gasped and looked at Albie, but he was looking carefully at Lady Howard.

"The Lenskeyn family jewels," he said softly.

Lady Howard nodded, looking discomforted. "They are yours now. They belong, rightfully, to the Countess of Lenskeyn."

"But they are yours by right," Albie protested. "My brother Elmore gave them to you, and you should keep them."

Theodosia could not agree more. *To take the presents of a man to his wife, now a widow...she could not countenance it.* She shut the lid and tried to press it back into her hands.

"I would rather you keep them," Lady Howard said gently. "Elmore died over a month ago, and...well. They belong to your family. I was only borrowing them, really."

She gently squeezed Theodosia's arm, curtseyed, and walked away.

Immediately, a footman approached them and bowed. "May I take that for you, your ladyship?"

It took a moment for Theodosia to realize who he was speaking to. "What—oh, yes. Please put them in a safe place, and I will consider what to do with them later."

Her mind was far more occupied with the lady who had just left them. "Albie, we should have Lady Howard—Elizabeth, isn't it? We should have Elizabeth stay with us."

Her husband nodded. He looked just as troubled as she felt. "Family is important. We should not let her be on her own, not at the moment."

They would undoubtedly have talked more if the dowager countess had not chosen that particular moment to accost them.

"Well," she said with a barely concealed sneer. "I see you have just received the Lenskeyn jewels. They were mine once, you know."

Theodosia swallowed and curtseyed low. She had neither seen nor spoken to the woman since that rather unfortunate altercation in the Assembly Rooms and was not entirely sure she trusted her tongue.

"I hope you are happy, now you have everything you want," she said.

And then Theodosia knew exactly what to say.

"Now look here, Mother," Albie began.

"Yes, I am happy," Theodosia said calmly. "And I have everything I want. A fine husband, and…and a family to come."

The older woman glared. "Yes, you can hope. Lady Elmore Howard hoped. No child came."

Theodosia placed a hand on her stomach. "Well, I have hope, and you may have more than hope in…what did Doctor Sanders say, Albie? Seven months? Perhaps six?"

For a moment, the dowager countess stared. The words did not seem to have sunk in.

Then she smiled, the gesture lighting up her face. "You cannot tell me—you do not mean to say…?"

"And it is to be kept quiet," said Albie hurriedly, and Theodosia knew why he wished to keep those particular dates quiet. *It would never do for society to know that the future Lord or Lady Howard was conceived just a little before their parents' wedding.* "But of course, we wanted you to be the first to know."

"Oh, I am so happy," his mother said unexpectedly—and she really looked it, too. "An heir! A continuation of the Lenskeyn line, oh you clever girl! Did you know at the Assembly Rooms? Tell me—"

"Not now, mother," said Albie firmly, for which Theodosia was grateful. She was not entirely sure she could face much more continued conversation with his mother. "Now, we must circulate and speak to our guests. We will see you later."

"Thank you," she whispered to him as they walked, arm in arm, across the hall. "For a moment there, I thought—"

"Ah, Miss Ashbrooke," smiled Miss Worsley, approaching them with a smile. "Or—what is the correct address for a countess? Your Grace?"

"Your ladyship," answered Theodosia automatically and smiled. "I will probably always answer to Miss Ashbrooke, however. 'Tis a hard habit to break!"

"And now I see why you had no interest in conversing with me, all those weeks ago," said Miss Worsley, grinning at the earl.

"No offense was meant, of course," he said hastily. "My heart was already taken with another."

He smiled at Theodosia, who thought her heart would explode with the happiness it was attempting to contain.

She was with child, his child! Whether a girl or boy, it would be loved by them more fiercely, perhaps, than they loved each other.

A swoop of nausea rushed over her, and Theodosia gripped her husband's arm a little more tightly.

His eyes narrowed. "And when was the last time you had something to drink?"

"I cannot remember—"

Albie snorted. "You must excuse me, Miss Worsley, I need to ensure my wife has something to drink, and my damned servants do not seem to understand that."

She smiled as he stormed off. *Bad habits or not, there was no one like Albie for attempting to protect her.*

With him gone, she looked shrewdly at Miss Worsley. "You strike me as someone not on the hunt for a husband, Miss Worsley. Am I correct?"

Miss Worsley laughed. "Not particularly—why have a husband when the world is changing? Much of why a husband would protect me, I can now protect myself. There is a new world coming, Miss— apologies, your ladyship, and I see no need for a man to have to hold my hand while I live in it. Besides, for all you know, I could be engaged already."

Theodosia nodded thoughtfully. She did not know Miss Worsley overly well, but she had read *Hamlet* before.

'The lady doth protest too much, methinks...'

"In that case," she said delicately as Albie returned with a glass of water in his hand, "you would not wish to meet Abraham Fitzclarence, Viscount Braedon?"

Her husband laughed. "Old habits die hard, I see!"

"Perhaps," smiled Theodosia. "But I am looking forward to making new habits with you."

She turned back to continue her conversation with Miss Worsley, but she had already drifted away.

"Good," said Albie, kissing her hand as he passed her the water. "Now get that down you. If you do not look after yourself, I will just have to do it for you."

Theodosia sipped the cool water and felt her whole body grow with affection. "I love you, winner of my heart."

"And I love you," Albie said, a mischievous grin growing, "matchmaker of my soul."

About Emily E K Murdoch

If you love falling in love, then you've come to the right place.

I am a historian and writer and have a varied career to date: from examining medieval manuscripts to designing museum exhibitions, to working as a researcher for the BBC to working for the National Trust.

My books range from England 1050 to Texas 1848, and I can't wait for you to fall in love with my heroes and heroines!

Follow me on twitter and instagram @emilyekmurdoch, find me on facebook at facebook.com/theemilyekmurdoch, and read my blog at www.emilyekmurdoch.com.

Made in the USA
Columbia, SC
13 March 2022

57587649R00124